Y FICTION HAL

Hale, Marian.

The truth about sparrows

Please check all items for damages
before leaving the Library.
Thereafter you will be held
responsible for all injuries
to items beyond reasonable wear.

THE TRUTH ABOUT
Sparrows

THE TRUTH ABOUT
Sparrows

MARIAN HALE

HENRY HOLT AND COMPANY
NEW YORK

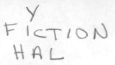

FICTION
HAL

MY DEEPEST GRATITUDE TO EACH OF THE FOLLOWING PEOPLE:
My parents, June and Robert Freeze, for their immutable love
and faith in me. Randall Wright, for his internal compass and
pivotal advice. My agent, Melanie Colbert, for believing in me
even before I knew. My editor, Reka Simonsen, for her impeccable
insight. The *Aransas Pass Progress* for allowing me to read their
fragile 1933 newspapers. Cathy Freeze, whose early critiques still
guide me. Barton Hill, whose writer's voice reminds me always of
what is possible. Heather Miller, Julie Hannah, Carla Ohlhausen,
Joan Holub, Beth Woods, Steve Miller, the Rockport Writer's
Group, and my children, Aliisa, Micah, and Allison, for their
candid feedback, unfailing support, and welcome cheers.

And a special thanks to my husband, Wendel, my ballast, my heart.

Henry Holt and Company, LLC, *Publishers since 1866*
115 West 18th Street, New York, New York 10011
www.henryholt.com

Henry Holt is a registered trademark of Henry Holt and Company, LLC
Copyright © 2004 by Marian Hale

Library of Congress Cataloging-in-Publication Data
Hale, Marian.
The truth about sparrows / Marian Hale.—1st ed.
260 p. cm.
Summary: Twelve-year-old Sadie promies that she will always be Wilma's best friend
when their families leaves drought-stricken Missouri in 1933, but once in Texas,
Sadie learns that she must try to make a new home—and new friends, too.
ISBN 0-8050-7584-4
EAN 978-0-8050-7584-7
1. Friendship—Fiction. 2. Moving, Household—Fiction. 3. Family life—Texas—Fiction.
4. Depressions—1929—Fiction. 5. People with physical disabilities—Fiction.
6. Texas—History—20th century—Fiction. I. Title.
PZ7.H1373Tr2004   [Fic]—dc22   2003056981

First Edition—2004 / Book designed by Patrick Collins
Printed in the United States of America on acid-free paper. ∞

1   3   5   7   9   10   8   6   4   2

In memory of:

My grandparents, Marian and J. D. Palmer,
who remain my measure for all that is dear

My brother, Bradley Freeze,
whose generous heart teaches me still

My grandson, Jacob Ryan Hale, our light

And all those who have lived in the shadow
of the Aransas Pass seawall

THE TRUTH ABOUT
Sparrows

Chapter One

I TURNED TWELVE on July 18, 1933, the day we left Missouri. Mama said there'd be no cake this year. She said I was getting a whole new life for my birthday instead, like I was being born all over again. I didn't care about the cake, but I sure didn't want a new life. My old one suited me just fine.

We were leaving Missouri 'cause Daddy couldn't make a living there as a mechanic anymore. Not as a carpenter, either. I asked him why, and he said, "When farmers suffer, Sadie, everyone suffers."

The drought had sucked the land dry, and it threatened to suck us dry, too, if we didn't get away. So Daddy sold our house for what he could get—a piddling amount, Mama called it—and we were up before daylight, squeezing our belongings into the car.

Daddy said he wanted to be on the road before the sun could shrivel one more blade of grass. But even the black of early morning felt hot enough to do that. Sweat crawled all over me like ants, and my damp dress clung to my legs while I worked. There didn't seem to be enough dark in the world to cool off the heat our land soaked up every day.

We packed Daddy's books—Charles Dickens and Daniel Defoe, Herman Melville and James Fenimore Cooper—the dozens of adventures he'd read to us chapter by chapter as far back as I could remember. We stuffed them into crates with the pots and bedding and tied everything to the car roof and down the running boards. Everything but the furniture. It didn't matter much that our beds and chairs sat in bare rooms waiting for new owners, but I hated leaving the table behind. I knew Mama did, too. Daddy had built that shiny drop-leaf table himself and given it to Mama the day they got married. She promised it'd be mine someday. I never knew Mama to break a promise.

I went back inside to see if she'd finished with the kitchen and found her wiping down the stove. Her hands looked pale as a new moon against the black iron, and her belly, slightly rounded with the new baby, rubbed against the stove edge. Long strands of dark hair, loose from their pins, swung with the rhythm of her cleaning. Seeing her shine everything for someone else made my stomach turn sour. I shoved back my own dark hair, sticky with sweat, and felt anger heat up my cheeks. She could've talked to Daddy, like I asked her to. She could've reminded him of how wearisome a trip could be and about the baby she lost when me and Jacob were little. If she had, we might not be leaving.

I ducked my head and ran a finger around the smooth edge of the table, too mad at Mama to look at her anymore. It wasn't fair we had to give up so much. My bitterness must've pushed a scowl onto my face 'cause Mama leaned close and whispered, "Daddy said he'd make us another table, Sadie. For our new life."

I nodded, but I knew it'd never be the same.

When we'd loaded all we could, three-year-old Bobby crawled into the front seat beside Daddy. I waited outside for Mama and took a last look toward the withered fields. I couldn't see much in the dark, but it didn't matter. I'd never get the picture of stunted grain, broken and spent, out of my head. I'd heard wind rattle through their papery bones so long I couldn't remember what quiet, green days were like anymore. I turned, skimmed the empty grain silos, and squinted down the road toward town. The halo of light on the horizon, faithful as the rising sun, was gone now. No one lit the street lamps in town anymore.

Nothing had been the same for a long time. Especially since Wilma left last month. The drought took everything from her family, too, like it did the Fosters, the Sullingers, and the Varners. Wilma was luckier than most, though. She knew where she was going. Family in California had offered to take them in, and she'd given me their address. We promised to write every day till we could see each other again.

I glanced east and saw clouds tinged with pink and purple. The sun would be up soon, and by midmorning, the brown fields and meadows would hum with heat. But I'd be gone by then. There'd be no more swimming in the river. No more purple fingers from ripe dewberries. And never again would I have a friend as good as Wilma to tell my thoughts to.

I turned my back on the parched land and climbed into the backseat beside five-year-old Emily. Her eyes shone from beneath her bangs, and she grinned at me, too excited about the trip to understand what we were giving up. Jacob, who was ten, wiggled between Emily and the window and set her to whining. He looked at me and shrugged, like it embarrassed him some that he was happy about the move and I wasn't.

Daddy was ready to leave, but Mama pulled the broom from the running board of the car and headed for the porch, determined to leave it clean. Sweeping seemed a waste of time to me. The wind was bound to get up like it did every day and blow the dusty yard onto the porch again. But Mama didn't care. She said the house had given its best and deserved no less from us.

She swept the dirt from under the porch swing and down the steps, then turned toward the house, staring. I couldn't tell what she was looking at. The patched holes in the screen door, maybe. The one halfway up, Jacob made with his cane pole. And the two down low, our hound started when she was chased by a swarm of bees. The next day, poor old Ruby died in Mama's arms from all the stings. We buried her in the backyard, and Emily cried 'cause we didn't have flowers for her grave. I cried, too, but not for lack of flowers.

Mama set our house key on the door ledge for the new owners. I looked away and saw Daddy turn his head, too. I knew he was sad. Last night, I heard Mama tell him, "All four of our babies took their first steps in this house."

He wasn't sad enough to stay, though.

Mama shoved the broom back down the running board, behind the camp stove, and climbed into the car. After a last look at the house, she nodded, and we headed down the road.

I tried hard not to be mad about leaving, but my feelings bucked all over the place. Home disappeared behind us, looking crisp-fried like Mama's hash brown potatoes, and all I could think about was how you can't start a new life without the old one dying first.

Chapter Two

WHEN IT GOT LIGHT ENOUGH to see, I pulled out the notebook paper Mama had given me and started a letter to Wilma. My pencil zigged and zagged with every bump in the road, but the writing made me feel better. I pretended I was having a real conversation with her, and I did fine till I remembered how my stomach rolled and sank that awful day we overheard our daddies talking in the kitchen.

Me and Wilma had worked up a thirst jumping rope in my backyard. We pumped fresh water at the well and sat down near the kitchen to cool off in the shade of a big sycamore tree. A dry wind got up, sparking dust devils, and soon it swept her daddy's voice through the screen door.

"I got the notice," Mr. Beldon said. "The bank's taking my house tomorrow, John. My land, too."

"I didn't know," I whispered.

Wilma stiffened beside me, but didn't say a word. She moved closer, instead, crouching beside the screen so she could catch every word.

"Have you and Mae decided where you're going?" I heard Daddy ask.

"Not many choices," Mr. Beldon said.

"California?"

Wilma's fingers, clammy and cold, groped for my hand and held tight.

"Mae's brother said he could take us in for a while," Mr. Beldon said. His voice sounded thick, achy with misery. "We'll pack what we can and head west in the morning."

Wilma sucked in a breath and stared at me like she'd just seen the end of the world.

"Where you headin' to, John?"

I heard the rasp of Daddy's fingers across his chin stubble, a sure sign he was troubled. I leaned against the clapboard siding, fear knotting in my chest, and waited.

"We're thinking Texas," he said finally.

Daddy's words hit me hard. Like the time Jacob barreled into me, chasing a fly ball. Same as then, I doubled over, the air knocked right out of me.

Wilma jerked me away from the screen door and pulled me toward the road. Without a word to anyone, we ran all the way to the river.

Gasping, we reached the shady bank and slid to the ground.

"What are we gonna do?" she asked.

I shook my head. I had no answers.

Wilma's fingers twisted in the blue cloth of her dress, in and out, in and out. "The bank took everything." Her voice turned breathy with tears. "Our house, our land." She looked at me, eyes bleary, cheeks wet as on the day her granny Fern died of influenza. "This is the last time I'll ever see you, Sadie."

I nodded, too sick to answer. I wrapped my arms around her and cried, tangling my hands in her straw-blond hair.

Wind rustled leaves, and doves cooed. Locusts sang, and the river bubbled and churned its way downstream like nothing in this world would ever change.

But it had.

I blinked away my tears and pulled back to look at her. "We're best friends, Wilma. True sisters. Nothing will ever change that."

She bit her bottom lip and nodded. "But *California*, Sadie. And *Texas*?" Her face crumpled, and tears spilled down her cheeks again.

"We'll write," I said. "Every single day." But my words sounded feeble and hopeless even to me.

Her head snapped up, and she looked at me hard. "Promise, Sadie Wynn. Promise I'll always be your best friend."

I nodded and drew my fingers over my chest in a big X. "Cross my heart," I whispered, and felt the pledge settle in the deepest part of me. "You'll always be my best friend, Wilma. Always."

I'm not sure how long we sat there. Minutes trickled past, steady as the river, till we didn't dare stay longer. Wilma started off down the road, eyes red and swollen, and I watched till the blue of her dress blurred and finally disappeared.

That was the last time I saw Wilma.

I squeezed my eyes shut, but even now, a full month later, I could still see that empty road. I could smell the hard-packed dirt beneath my feet, see faded sunlight flickering through leaves at the road's edge, and feel again how I wished the river would swallow us up, hide us from what was coming. But most of all, I remembered the quiver in Wilma's voice when she said, "Promise, Sadie."

I folded my letter and put it away.

Daddy soon turned south and pointed the car toward the Texas coast. He said a lack of rain couldn't keep

< 10 >

a man from making a living there. Snow, either, 'cause it hardly ever snowed in South Texas. He said the warm Gulf bays were full of fish. And even though the house money wasn't much, there'd be enough after the trip to buy lumber for a small fishing boat. I knew Daddy was smart and a good planner. I knew, too, he could've found a way to stay in Missouri if he'd wanted to.

We rode every day of that trip wedged in the car, and every night we camped near rivers and streams. Me and Mama would set to work on supper right away while Emily and Bobby gathered firewood. Jacob helped Daddy set up the tent.

The closer we got to Texas, the more bugs there seemed to be. Ants and gnats and cockroaches—lots of cockroaches. Some of them were big. Sometimes they'd find their way into the tent at night and send us all scurrying till we got them out. Except for Daddy. He'd just lie there laughing at all the swatting and shuddering.

Most times, we saw other people camped along the rivers. They'd sleep on the ground or in tents, their belongings crammed into trucks or cars, just like us. And others carried their whole lives in a flour sack tucked under their arms.

Once, we met a man and his son traveling by foot to Louisiana.

"The boy's ma died a few weeks back," the man said. "If we can get to my sister's place, we'll be okay. There's work for me there."

Mama fed them, and when they left the next morning, she made sure the boy put extra bread in his pockets for the road.

Another time, a squabble broke out between two men. I couldn't tell about what. Before Mama could shoo us into the tent, I saw the bigger man duck away from a swinging tire iron. The end caught him on the cheek and flayed it open clear to the bone. Mama and Daddy didn't get much sleep that night, and before daylight, we packed up and headed out of there, back to the road again.

Two Sundays came and went without church. Mama didn't like the idea we'd be living like heathens till we were good and settled, but she was a practical woman. As long as Daddy gave us Bible verses to ponder, she didn't complain. I liked the verses better than church, anyway, though it was a puzzlement how Daddy seemed to know just what I needed to hear. I finally figured God must be seeing right down inside me and guiding Daddy's finger to the right verse.

Daddy didn't miss church at all. He fancied his Bible reading done under his own roof, or even better, under a blue sky. He said it didn't make a lick of sense to think the good Lord preferred to be locked away in a stuffy old church house all week and let loose just on Sundays. He said God was everywhere His word was. And even in places it wasn't.

Mama always frowned when Daddy got started on religion. But when I thought about it, I had to agree with him. Any fool able-minded enough to breathe could see God had to be everywhere. Shining in the new green of sprouted grain. Or dancing on the roof with the rain. Or fluttering in the blue shimmer of a dragonfly's wing. I didn't say much about it, though. I figured Mama might be happier if I kept those thoughts to myself.

It took us fifteen days to get to East Texas. After a hard day of flat tires, jabbing elbows, and weary spirits, we made camp early near the Sabine River. We had time to put a hook in the water, and that night we had fried fish to go with Mama's canned tomatoes and pan bread. After supper, Daddy pulled his drawstring bag of Bull Durham from his pocket, shook tobacco onto a square of paper, and rolled a cigarette. We cleaned up while he had his smoke, then we all crawled into the tent.

Every night, we slept laid out like cordwood on an old canvas wagon sheet to keep out the damp. Me on the outside, 'cause I was the oldest, Emily next to me, then Jacob. Bobby snuggled against Mama, but he woke me in the middle of the night, same as always, clutching his pants and calling, "Sadie, Sadie." I'd take him outside to pee, then squeeze him in next to me, where he'd sleep still as a possum till morning.

We didn't have to stop for much more than gasoline and flat tires on that trip. Daddy had stocked up on tire patches, and Mama had poked her jars of canned black-eyed peas and tomatoes everywhere. They rattled and clinked under the seats, between our feet, and inside her big pressure canner. It was enough to feed us for close to a month if we were careful. If Bobby hadn't lost our map in the river and Daddy hadn't taken a wrong turn, we would've never had to stop at that store. I guess that was the first time I really saw Daddy the way strangers saw him. Until then, I thought the world was full of daddies like mine.

We parked near the storefront and stirred up a cloud of dust that hung in the air thick as fog. I rubbed my stinging eyes and reached for the door, but Mama said no. Jacob and Emily huffed their disappointment. Bobby whined. I leaned back and turned my attention to the handful of men sitting on empty crates beside the screen door. They watched us, too, through the settling dust but kept on talking.

Daddy grabbed the handle on his open car door, swung himself out, and sat on the ground. The men hushed. Bags of tobacco gaped open, and cigarettes hung from their lips.

Daddy's shriveled lower legs lay folded in the dirt. He wore heavy socks on his twisted feet, and his shortened pant legs were tied up with cording. He wrapped it around his small calves and over his knees every morning to keep the extra cloth out of his way. I watched him lean forward and fix his palms in the dirt. Then, using his strong arms like crutches, he lifted himself off the ground, swung his body forward, and sat. Then he did it all over again. His dangling calves and feet trailed limp beneath him with each swinging stride.

The men never said a word, but their wide-eyed looks followed Daddy right through the screen door.

I'd never seen grown men gawk like that, but Daddy must have. I shrank from the sight and felt my face flush red, but he kept on going without a single glance around him.

Hard as I tried, I couldn't figure out those stares. Hadn't those men ever seen someone who couldn't use his legs? I looked at Mama, but her face didn't tell me a thing.

Back home, everyone knew Mr. Dayton's missing fingers made it troublesome to hold a fork. And Mr. Severn had a whole arm missing from the war. No one stared at them like those strangers stared at

< 15 >

Daddy. But then, everyone at home knew us. They knew Daddy was more than just a cripple.

Mama had told me the story about Daddy's useless legs a long time ago. As a little baby he'd been just like everyone else, till he got sick. The doctors called it infantile paralysis. It twisted his feet and shriveled his legs to half their size. He never got a chance to walk, but he learned early on how to get around. He could go just about anywhere he wanted. And if there were no way around a muddy place in the road, he'd just lean forward on his palms, sweep his shrunken legs into the air, and walk on his hands.

I asked Mama once why he didn't want a wheelchair. She shook her head and said, "Don't you ever ask your daddy that."

But I already knew better. I remembered Daddy chasing off a church committee that tried to make him their charity case for that year. He couldn't abide charity or pity. He was out the door before they could get their shiny new wheelchair unloaded, fussing all the way. He could move real fast when he wanted to.

I guess there wasn't anything Daddy couldn't do. He could carpenter and climb a ladder good as any walking man. He could swim, too. And there wasn't a car, truck, or tractor he couldn't fix. He built our car out of spare parts, mostly, and before we left for Texas, he rigged the foot pedals so he could work them with his hands.

I heard the screen door slam and saw Daddy come out of the store with a new map stuffed in his shirt pocket. His strong arms swung his body down the steps toward the car. He opened the door, put a hand on the steering wheel, and with one hard pull he hauled himself onto the seat. When we drove away, I was sure those men with their slack jaws and popped eyes would be staring at our dust till the middle of next week. I felt shame twisting at my insides, felt it push an awful heat into my cheeks, but I didn't know who I was mad at most. Those men would've had nothing to stare at if Daddy hadn't made us leave home.

I can't remember giving Daddy's crippled legs too much thought before that day. He always worked and came in for supper like everyone else. But I gave those men a lot of thought. I finally figured they had to be purely ignorant, or they would've shown more manners. I guessed I'd have to forgive them, but it was hard. They'd stirred something ugly in me, and I didn't even know if I could forgive myself.

Chapter Three

DADDY DROVE down the road a ways, then pulled to the side to study his new map. He said if we followed the Sabine River, it would lead us right to the Gulf of Mexico before nightfall.

By the time we got headed in the right direction, we were in good spirits. But all our squirming and giggling at the prospect of seeing a real ocean distracted Daddy from his driving something fierce. Mama got us still again by singing "Red River Valley" and "Church in the Wildwood." Me, Jacob, and Emily knew all the words, but Bobby would latch on to a line that caught his fancy and sing it over and over, whether it belonged or not.

When the day was half gone, Mama passed out dried figs and wedges of leftover pan bread spread with peanut butter. We ate riding down the road while Mama fed Daddy. He needed both hands to drive. After we ate, we played I Spy and Count the Windmills. I could spot more windmills than anyone else, and I would've won every time, too, if Daddy hadn't helped the other kids. I was quicker, being the oldest, and he always insisted on keeping things fair. Except maybe a time or two.

I squinted against the bright sunlight streaming through my car window and thought about the games me and Wilma liked to play. Checkers, jump rope, hopscotch, jacks. She always beat me at jacks, but I was real good at checkers—better than anyone 'cause Daddy sat with me so many times after supper, teaching me strategy. Wilma never had a chance.

Then there was the time me and Wilma begged to see *Dracula* starring Bela Lugosi at the picture show. Our mamas shook their heads and said ten-year-old girls had no business seeing that sort of thing, that we'd have nightmares for sure. But the next day, Daddy and Mr. Beldon had some trading to do in town, and they said we could go along for the ride. I remember Daddy winked at me when I got into the car, and Mr. Beldon held his finger to his lips like he had a big secret. They drove us straight to the Palace Theater, poked dimes in our hands, and let us out.

Huddled inside the dark theater, lights flickering across our faces, we saw the hideous Count Dracula bare his fangs. We covered our eyes while people all around us gasped and screamed. Later, hearts still thumping, we blinked in the bright sunlight, safe at last.

But that night, with the lamp out and everyone asleep but me, I had second thoughts. I had to admit that Mama might've been right. I didn't have nightmares, but I couldn't sleep for months without the covers pulled up to my chin and the windows closed. And poor Wilma got caught with garlic strung around her neck to ward off vampires. Her mama wasn't any too happy about that.

I guess Daddy hadn't been fair when he went against Mama's wishes so we could do what all the bigger kids were doing. But me and Wilma agreed it was the nicest thing our daddies had ever done for us. And despite all the sleepless nights, it was the most fun, too.

When the sun finally dipped behind the trees and I could open my eyes again, I spotted gleaming gray-and-white birds swooping overhead. I asked Daddy about them. He said they were seagulls and we'd be seeing lots of them from now on. Still full of remembering, I leaned back and listened to their calls. The sound stirred a loneliness in me that made my insides feel hollow. Like I'd lost more than a home and a best friend. Like I'd lost a piece of me I might not ever find again.

"Smell that?" Daddy asked.

I pushed my face into the wind. The first whiff reminded me of the salt brine Mama soaked her pickling cucumbers in. The next assured me that sea air was unlike anything I'd smelled before.

Daddy grinned at Mama. He cocked his head to one side and whispered, "Listen."

We got real still, straining to make out what Daddy heard over the chug of the car engine. He followed a winding road, and when we cleared the dunes, a surging roar rushed at us. Acres and acres of green water swelled and rolled, splashing white foam onto miles of shiny wet sand. I stared, hardly breathing. We were on the edge of the world without another soul in sight.

I hung out the window. Salt air billowed my shirt, ruffled my eyelashes, and whipped through my hair. Jacob and Emily pushed and shoved till they squeezed through the other window, shoulder to shoulder. When I tried to talk, the wind filled my mouth and puffed out my cheeks. Jacob tried to make fun of me, but it happened to him, too. I couldn't wait to tell Wilma about all this.

Daddy stopped the car, and Jacob ducked back in. He leaned over the front seat, his dark hair blown ever' which-a-way, his blue eyes full of sparkle and yearning. "Can we go swimming, Mama?" he asked. Mama had a hard time telling those eyes no, and he knew it.

Emily squeezed between Mama and him, and Jacob shot her a rankled look. "Please, Mama," she begged. "Say yes."

"Yes, yes, yes!" Bobby shouted, bouncing on the seat till jars rattled.

I watched for the break in Mama's expression, for the softening around her eyes and the sigh that meant she'd give in. But she shook her head instead.

"It'll be dark soon, and we have to find a place to camp and fix supper."

Jacob and Emily groaned and fell back onto the seat. But I saw Daddy pat Mama's knee. He leaned close and said, "We got water. We could camp here."

Mama looked up and down the empty beach, then turned and looked back at the dunes. I held my breath and waited.

After a long moment, Mama said, "Sadie, you're in charge. If anyone"—she paused and pointed a finger at us—"any *one* of you gets more than knee-deep, they'll get a whipping. Understood?"

Our heads bobbed, but Mama's eyes hadn't dismissed us yet. She had a look that could pin your feet to the floor when she was serious-minded. We looked back with all the wide-eyed reassurance we could muster and waited for her nod. When it came, we burst out of the car, whooping and hollering all the way to the water.

Around daybreak the next morning, Mama woke me up, grumbling. She moved our bowl of shells aside, shook sand out of her dress, then woke Daddy. She said she wouldn't fix another meal till we got someplace we could wash up. Daddy laughed, but he didn't argue. Mama dug out her jar of dried figs and passed them around.

Though I was hungry for more than figs, I was ready to go, too. My skin felt sticky and gritty from the swim yesterday. And the salty Gulf water had left my hair so matted, I could barely get a comb through it. I began to wonder if all this misery was penance for my anger at having to leave home.

While I tugged a comb through the tangled mess around my face, Daddy opened his Bible for our morning verse. He had a slight grin on his face.

"Ecclesiastes," he said. "Chapter seven, verse nine. 'Be not hasty in thy spirit to be angry, for anger resteth in the bosom of fools.'" He slapped the book closed, handed it to Mama, and began taking down the tent.

I couldn't tell if he'd aimed that verse at Mama's impatience or at me for my bitterness at having to leave home, but I took Daddy's words to heart. God might've whispered them to him especially for me. And though I still had a hankering for Mama's fat pancakes, I accepted another dried fig with a humble thank-you and vowed to be more forgiving.

Daddy drove down the road a piece till we came on a windmill close enough to get to. He sat in the car while we climbed through a barbed-wire fence, rinsed off in a cattle trough, and tromped back through the brush. Mama brought back a wet rag so Daddy could wash up, too. With her dark hair dripping but freshly combed, she looked happy at last.

Over the next few days, we followed the Texas coast past Freeport, Port Lavaca, and Rockport. The moist Gulf air sat heavy in my chest, but the breezes made the hot days feel cooler than back home.

Daddy still hadn't decided where we'd end up. He'd read about Corpus Christi and said we might head there first. But out past Aransas Pass and Ingleside, we got into cotton country, and things changed.

Daddy drove slow, studying workers in the fields. Sun-browned men and women—kids, too—bent over rows of cotton, working in the hot sun. Their rag-wrapped fingers pulled white puffs from bushy plants and stuffed them into bags looped over their shoulders. It looked like it'd take an awful lot of picking to fill those long bags.

Daddy stopped. He got out of the car and went

into the field to talk to the men. I couldn't hear their words, but I could see their faces. They gave Daddy the same gawking looks those strangers did at that store. After talking a bit, one of the men pulled cotton from a sun-baked plant and handed it to Daddy. Then he pointed across the field to where big wagons sat—some empty, some brimming with cotton. Daddy nodded, shook their hands, and came back to the car. He pulled the cotton out of his pocket and handed it to Mama. She looked at it and passed it back to us. "Did they think we could get on?" she asked.

He nodded, and I felt my stomach tighten up. Daddy had never been one to miss an opportunity to make money or learn something new.

Emily punched Jacob and gave him an excited look. "We're gonna pick cotton," she whispered.

I glared at the endless fields, at the kids tugging big bags behind them, working beside their mamas and daddies. It looked like hot, mean work to me, and I didn't relish the thought of putting up with more gaping, wide-eyed looks from strangers.

I stared hard at Daddy. There was no way around it. Just when I thought I might forgive him for making us leave home, I found out he'd lied to us about the fishing. I'd given up my very best friend and the only home I'd ever had to spend the rest of my days picking cotton.

Chapter Four

DADDY PULLED right into the cotton fields, down a narrow dirt road, and stopped in a clearing near the wagons. He got out and talked to the boss while we waited in the car with Mama. The man had a fierce look of doubt on his face, but he soon shrugged and pointed to some buildings at the far edge of the fields. They looked like apple crates hunkered under the hot sun.

The man handed a stack of folded bags to Daddy and stood back to watch. Daddy looped the straps of each bag over his shoulder, pulled them behind him to the car, and pitched them in to Mama. Then he hauled himself onto the front seat. The man's eyebrows lifted. He shook his head and turned back to his work.

"We'll start after the noon meal," Daddy said. He pointed to the apple-crate buildings. "We're to stay out there."

Mama nodded.

We headed down the dirt road, but the nearer we got to those little houses, the harder Mama's face looked. A dozen one-room cabins sat spittin'-close to one another. The board siding gaped, leaving little chance of privacy, and the only cabin that was empty leaned on its blocks like it was tuckered out. Mama stepped in, glanced around at the mounds of blown-in dirt and weeds, and stepped out. "We'll stay in the tent," she said.

Mama picked a place off to one side near a scrub oak, and we hurried to set up camp. Out in the fields, workers dropped their cotton bags. Some pulled towel-wrapped meals from their overalls and ate where they were, leaning against half-filled sacks. Others walked back to the cabins. By the time they trickled in, Daddy had fired up the coal-oil stove and Mama had pancake batter sizzling in a hot skillet. We wouldn't have time for pan bread today. She flipped the cakes out, sprinkled them with a bit of sugar, and rolled them up. The sugared pancakes tasted good, but they did little to sweeten my sour thoughts.

I ate under the tree and watched men gather in the sliver of shade cast by the cabins. They sat in the dirt and leaned against the warped siding while women and kids disappeared through open doorways to fetch their meals. Seemed like all of them stole curious glances at us. I wondered if my growing vexation showed on my face, but I should've known it was Daddy they were looking at. A few men nodded our way, and Daddy nodded back.

When we finished eating, Mama wrapped each one of our fingers with narrow strips of rags so the prickly cotton bolls wouldn't tear up our hands. Except for Bobby. He got a spoon and a wooden bowl for digging in the dirt. Mama handed Jacob his hat and told us girls to put on our bonnets. "Stay close to Daddy," she said. "He'll show us how it's done."

Jacob and Emily followed Daddy into the field with their long bags, but I dug my toes into the hot dirt and waited for Mama. She tied her bonnet with bandaged fingers and pulled Bobby toward the field. I should've kept my mouth shut, but I knew I'd bust like an overripe melon if I didn't say something. I fell into step, drew a deep breath, and spit it out. "Did Daddy lie to us, Mama?"

She stopped and frowned hard at me. The look made my gut tighten up, but I was determined. I jerked my slipping bag back over my shoulder. "He promised we'd live on the coast and fish, Mama, and here we are in a cotton field."

She shook her head and gave me a look that made me feel small and mean. "Your daddy's a smart man, Sadie. He's here for more than just pay."

Mama pulled Bobby into the field and left me standing in the dirt. I hadn't thought it was possible to feel worse, but I did.

I don't remember much about those five days except for the hot, achy work and wondering what Daddy was here for if it wasn't the money. At dusk, everyone came in from the fields too tired for socializing, so I knew Daddy wasn't here for that. But like Mama said, I could tell he wanted more. Every evening he sat outside the tent like he was waiting for something. It wasn't till the last night that I understood what it was.

While me and Mama washed up supper dishes, a few workers drifted our way. Daddy shook their hands and introduced himself. "My name's John Wynn," he said. He nodded at Mama. "And my wife here is Raine."

Mama smiled her hello. Her name was really Lorraine, but Daddy liked Raine better. One day I asked him why, and he said there was nothing in this world sweeter than rain, and Mama wasn't much different.

The men talked with Daddy awhile, then more came with wives and kids. Mama made coffee, and me and Emily played hopscotch by lamplight with a green-eyed girl named Dollie Mae Gillem. She was thin and wiry with freckles and short curly red hair, the only girl in a family of six boys, and nothing at all like Wilma. Her steady stream of chatter left me wondering if she'd pass out from lack of air.

She told me about all she had to put up with, being the only girl in the family, and pointed out three of her brothers huddled around a game of marbles. "There's Davis—he's thirteen and the oldest—and that's Oren and Wyatt next to him," she said.

I saw Jacob smack in the middle of them, hunched over a circle drawn in the sand.

"Mama's holding baby Caleb," she said, "and over there, that's Ethan and Tanner." She pointed out the last two Gillems playing tag with Bobby and a few others. They chased around the tent, hollering and laughing so hard their mamas had to put their cups aside to settle them down.

Daddy sat on the ground, his crippled legs folded sideways, out of the way. He talked to those men like he wasn't any different at all. And soon they talked back like they didn't see his crippled legs anymore. Always quick, he caught me looking and smiled. Daddy had a handsome smile, and I felt it swell inside me like a clean breath.

For a while, the grown-up talk took on a festive

mood. Seemed like we were all glad to be done with the cotton and looked forward to collecting our pay first thing in the morning. I hoped Daddy would bring out his fiddle, but he must've had more important things on his mind. I caught snatches of talk about the Depression, about looking for work and the worry of feeding hungry kids. A woman, her dress hanging slack over her whisper-thin body, cheeks shining wet, listened at lamp's edge. She clutched a rag doll to her chest like a baby, and I had to wonder at the kind of misfortune that put such a sorrowful look on her face. Even with all we gave up, I guessed we might've been luckier than some.

Before long, Emily tired of playing hopscotch and wandered off. Dollie balanced on one foot, watching her go, then threw down her rock. She grabbed a spare cotton bag and pulled me away from the light.

"Finally," she said. "Now we can be alone. Would you like to sit down and talk? You have a real sweet sister, Sadie, and Lord knows I'd love to have one just like her instead of all those brothers, but I've been dying to get you all to myself. She's only five, after all, and it's hard to speak your mind with a little one around."

Dollie spread the bag, sat on one end, and looked up at me. "Come on," she said. "Don't you want to get to know each other?" Not waiting for an answer, she patted the space beside her and kept talking while I sat down.

"I've never seen anyone with hair dark as yours paired up with blue eyes and white skin," she said. "Papa would say you're a beauty, that's for sure." She smoothed her wild curls with her hand, but they popped right back up. "I'd trade you if I could, but I guess I'm gonna be stuck with this red mop the rest of my days."

I fingered one of my thick pigtails and stared at her. I couldn't remember anyone describing me as a beauty before. I felt my cheeks color up, but Dollie didn't notice. She kept on talking, telling me about how she'd come from Ohio two years ago, and how out of all the places they'd tried to settle along the way, she liked South Texas best. She talked about what it was like living by the bay, and how much she missed having a friend her age in the neighborhood. Clumps of red hair bobbed as she spoke, and though she asked dozens of questions, she never waited for answers. She prattled on and on about the things we could do together if only I lived close by.

I didn't say much. Even if I'd wanted to squeeze in a word or two, it seemed a waste of time, seeing as how our families would scatter in different directions in the morning. Besides, I already had a best friend, and I had no intention of breaking my promise to Wilma.

While Dollie rambled on, I wondered what Wilma would think. I smiled, already hearing that hiccuping guffaw of hers. She'd laugh for sure—but more at me than at Dollie, for letting myself get cornered and corralled.

I couldn't do much about Dollie's endless chatter, any more than I could've stopped Daddy from moving. But after a while, I figured I could do something about my listening.

I stood up right in the middle of a story about a girl named Lou Ann Waller, who wanted to get away from the smell of fish and shrimp so bad she threatened to run off with her boyfriend. "I'd better get back," I said. "Mama doesn't know where I am."

Dollie looked up, surprised, but it didn't seem to bother her none. She gathered up the cotton bag and followed me to the tent.

When we got back, everyone was shaking Daddy's hand and wishing us well. All but the Gillems. They stayed a bit longer.

Once they were finally gone, Mama shooed us off to bed while she and Daddy sat in the starlight, talking. We didn't complain. I was bone-tired by then and knew the other kids were, too. Bobby fell asleep right away, and it wasn't long before Jacob's and Emily's breathing turned slow and steady, too. But tired as I was, I couldn't sleep. I lay there by the open tent flap, watching the red glow from Daddy's cigarette and listening to his hushed voice tell Mama all the things he'd learned from those men.

"In Aransas Pass, there's a big dirt seawall by the harbor," he said, "built to keep storm tides from washing the town away. We can camp there free."

"The owners won't care, John?" Mama asked.

"There don't seem to be any owners. People all over the country bought those lots in a big land auction in 1909 and never showed up to claim them."

I waited for Mama's voice. Daddy must've been waiting, too, 'cause I didn't hear a word for a while. When Daddy spoke again, it was in a whisper. "The harbor's close there, Raine, and the fishing's good."

I knew neither of them liked living on someone else's land. But I knew, too, Daddy was thinking about how hard it'd be to get to and from his boat every day.

Still, Mama was quiet.

"Dan Gillem said he and Irene are going back there tomorrow, and we could go with them."

I sucked in a surprised breath and was thankful when the sound disappeared under Mama's sigh and the rasp of Daddy's rough hand rubbing her shoulders.

"Might be a good place to settle," Daddy said.

I rolled over, finally understanding what it was he'd hoped to find in these cotton fields. I'd found something, too, whether I wanted it or not. I was getting my new life, just like Mama said, but it was coming ready-made with a chattering redheaded girl who wanted to be my friend. A girl who didn't know I had a promise to keep.

< 35 >

Chapter Five

THE NEXT MORNING Mr. Gillem's truck, loaded with kids and gear, led us through Aransas Pass. The trip through town had Jacob's head swiveling left to right and back again, trying to read all the signs.

"Hander's Gas Station," he read. "The Bakery Café. Aw, I bet they don't make biscuits good as yours, Mama. Rexall Drugstore, and— Hey!" Jacob stuck his head out the window. "New Chevrolets!"

We passed Snyder and Clark Chevrolet, and Jacob gaped out the back window at the shiny new cars till we turned east and he couldn't see them anymore.

Up ahead, I saw the seawall. It looked like a pale green snake stretched out in the sun, but when we got closer, the dusty green turned to cedar trees.

"Planted close," Daddy said, "to keep the wall from washing away."

We followed Mr. Gillem over a railroad track, up the crushed oyster-shell road, and over the top of the seawall. The road took a sharp left, and we found ourselves sandwiched between the wall and the harbor. A long row of fish houses squatted over the water, grasping at the road like they'd fall in if they didn't hang on tight—Minter's Fish House, Colter's, Collins's, and more. I could see clean through them to the green water on the other side. I didn't see many people around, but fat cats stretched and curled under empty tables and in doorways, waiting for scraps from the day's catch. Daddy said things probably picked up fast when the boats came back every evening.

I smelled tarred dock pilings heating up under the sun and saw a boat sunk right there in the harbor with only its cabin and mast showing. And when we passed Ma Beasley's Café, I heard "Ain't She Sweet" coming from the lighted jukebox just inside the door. The music faded under the clank of hammering, and next door, I saw freshly dipped nets. Some lay spread out on the ground to dry, while others hung from tall racks, still dripping tar into barrels beneath them. Then the hammering stopped, and steam licked the door ledge of Roy Guire's blacksmith shop.

When we'd seen it all, Mr. Gillem led us back over

the seawall. He made a quick turn to the right, pulled onto a narrow, one-car lane that looked more like a trail than a road, and drove between two rows of tents and little houses. They were nothing more than shanties, really, built from scraps and covered with tar paper. Some sat snuggled against the dirt seawall, still shaded from the new day; others sat across from them, laid bare to the August sun. He stopped not far from the road, in front of a little house covered in black paper and roofed with rusty tin. I didn't see how a family of nine could fit inside such a small space, but they seemed happy to be home. Daddy pulled up not far from them and said we'd be camping right there tonight, thanks to our new friends.

Mr. Gillem unfolded his lanky body, stepped from the truck, and walked around to the other side to help Mrs. Gillem with the baby. It was easy to see where Dollie got her looks. She was small like her mama, but that red hair came from her daddy. His red curls crawled all over his head and onto his face like a great lion's mane. Mrs. Gillem kept her chestnut braids wrapped around her head. She handed Caleb to Mr. Gillem, jumped from the truck, and almost disappeared from sight. It didn't seem possible that her short, doll-like frame could've birthed seven kids.

Before I could get out of the car, Dollie came running up with her ten-year-old brother, Oren.

"Hey, Pollywog!" Davis hollered from the truck bed. "Come on back here. You and Oren got work to do."

Dollie put her hands on her hips and scowled her irritation. "I told you not to call me that, Davis."

Davis flashed a grin full of straight white teeth and winked at me like he was sure I'd find his teasing funny. I looked away quick, but my cheeks flushed hot. When Oren pointed at me and laughed, I felt the color in my face deepen.

"Don't pay 'im no mind," Dollie said. "Ever since Davis filled in for that injured deckhand on the *Nancy Sue* last week, he's been strutting like a peacock, trying to act big as the rest of them shrimpers. Mama keeps telling him that pride goeth before a fall, but he won't listen."

The boys were hard to ignore. I didn't like the arrogant way Davis winked at me, and I didn't like being made fun of. I glared hard at Oren. He blinked, looked embarrassed, and then tried to pretend nothing had happened.

"Mama said we could help the Wynns set up camp," Dollie hollered at Davis.

Before I could send her older brother a warning look, she asked, "Do you think that's okay?"

I glanced at Mama, and she nodded.

With a quick grin, Dollie grabbed a box from the floorboard, and Oren helped Jacob with the tent. When I looked back at the truck, Davis was gone.

The Gillem kids weren't afraid of work. We settled quicker than ever, even with Dollie's chatter, and ate our noon meal early so Daddy could leave with Mr. Gillem to see about boats. Bobby played with Ethan and Tanner, and the bigger boys scattered—Jacob with them. But I heard Mama tell him to get back soon 'cause there was work to do. I figured it had to be the washing. We were out of clean clothes, and there'd be water to haul.

Mama sat with Mrs. Gillem in the snippet of shade behind the house while little Caleb nursed. I heard them talking about heading and peeling shrimp at the fish houses on the harbor road and at another place close by called Rice Cannery. Mr. Gillem usually did both, leaving when the cannery whistle called at four in the morning and going on to the fish houses when the boats came in every evening. Older kids like Davis worked at the cannery, too, off and on.

Emily sat alone by the tent, looking as lost as I felt. Dollie spotted her and elbowed me. "Ain't she a cutie? She looks just like a carnival Kewpie doll with those chubby cheeks. I hate to see her so sad, though. It's not fair we all got someone and she doesn't."

Dollie marched up to Emily, grabbed her hand, and pulled her to her feet. "Willa Dean Pickens is five just like you," she said. "If her mama's not working at the cannery, she'll be playing outside."

Emily gave me a happy smile, and her chipmunk cheeks pushed her eyes into half-moons.

Dollie got permission for a short walk and took off with Emily between the two rows of houses. I followed, though my heart wasn't in it, picking my way across hot, salt-crusted sand.

When Dollie wasn't telling us about the people living in each house or tent, she was pointing out blue herons and sandpipers, dogs and cats. She nodded toward a tiny one-room house built close to the seawall and surrounded by big red hibiscus bushes in full bloom. "That's Mr. Caughlin's place," she said. A garden sat close by, turned under except for tall stalks of okra. Beyond was a chicken pen and an outhouse. "He taught his dog to grin," Dollie said, "and sometimes he gives us watermelon or cherry tomatoes. And once he had a pet badger he used to take for walks in the evenings. He's real nice."

Lou Ann Waller lived next door and spent most of her days babysitting for her working mama. I remembered Dollie telling me how the fifteen-year-old girl preferred dirty diapers to being stuck at the cannery every morning.

The Haukes, on the left, had electric lights. "But Mrs. Hauke won't let anyone else listen to their radio," Dollie said. "Mama says it's 'cause God didn't give her children that she's so stingy." She stopped and leaned close. "But sometimes all us kids sit down-wind in the dark and listen. *The Grand Ole Opry, Amos 'n' Andy, The Lone Ranger.*" She grinned. "You can hear every word if you're quiet."

We turned around at the end of the trail and headed back. Emily dragged her feet, disappointed that we didn't find Willa Dean, but Dollie told her we'd try again.

"I know every family this side of the tracks," she said, "and before long, you'll know 'em, too."

Seagulls squawked overhead, salt-crusted sand burned my feet, and everywhere I looked, I saw nothing but shacks.

I missed our house, with the porch swing Daddy built and the big sycamore tree out back. I missed Mama's Sunday apple cake, my soft bed, and even sunlight glinting off the old grain silos. Without them, I didn't know who I was anymore.

But mostly I missed Wilma. If she were here, she'd see right away we didn't belong in this place. We belonged in Missouri.

Chapter Six

WHEN I GOT BACK from our walk, Mama had her iron pot half full of water and heating over a campfire. "We'll be buying water from Mrs. Kendall like the Gillems do," she said.

"I'd be happy to show Sadie where to fill the buckets, Mrs. Wynn," Dollie offered.

Mama shook her head. "Thank you, Dollie, but there's no need. Jacob and Oren are taking care of it."

I saw the boys walking easy-like down the road with a full bucket in each hand, their pants already dark with sloshed water. Mrs. Kendall lived close, but it must've seemed awfully far carrying that much water. Mama set the washtub on the storage box we used for a worktable and stood aside while the boys emptied their buckets.

"More?" Jacob asked.

Mama slid the scrub board into the water and pointed to a larger tub sitting on the ground, the one we used for baths. "At least one more trip for the rinsing," she said. "And don't forget to fill the water barrel, too."

The boys sighed and headed back with their empty buckets.

Mrs. Gillem stepped outside and called Dollie home to chores. It was just as well. I surely didn't need someone chattering at my elbow while I was trying to get the wash done.

When the water was near boiling, Mama dropped in the white clothes, a piece at a time, and I stirred them into the soapy water. After a bit, I pulled them out with a stick and pushed them into the tub of cool water for scrubbing. Daddy's denim pants, dirtier than anything else, were the last to go in the pot and the longest at the scrub board. When the clothes looked clean, I wrung them out and placed them in the larger tub for rinsing.

By the time we were done, my red hands ached. Mrs. Gillem had insisted we use her clothesline till we got one of our own—their outhouse, too. But we'd started late, and the sun sat low in the sky by the time we got the clothes hung out back to dry.

They'd have to be left overnight and gathered in tomorrow.

Daddy came back shortly after we finished. He had a folded piece of paper stuffed in his shirt pocket, and a carpenter's rule sticking out of his back pocket. He sat in the tent's growing shade and studied his list of measurements while Mama poured him a cup of coffee.

I sat beside him, peering at a half-drawn picture at the bottom of the page. "Is that our new boat?" I asked.

He nodded, but before I could ask more questions, Mama called me. "Take this coffee to Daddy," she said, "then come help me start supper."

I did as I was told, but I longed to see more of what Daddy was working on. Back home, I'd always been fascinated at how he could puzzle pieces of lumber into a building.

I peeled the potatoes and onions while Mama floured and browned the last of her canned duck. Then I glanced at Daddy. He was drawing.

I poured the chopped onions and potatoes over the duck.

Daddy pulled out another piece of paper.

I stirred while Mama drew water from the barrel to cover the meat and vegetables.

Daddy's brow wrinkled over new figures.

Mama put a lid on the pot and started biscuits.

I cleaned up the flour mess quick as I could and sat back down beside Daddy to see what he'd gotten done.

Sections of his boat, complete with measurements, were drawn all over his paper. I saw words I didn't understand, like *stem, rib,* and *chine,* but then I'd never seen plans for a boat before. I remembered Mama telling me once that Daddy could figure lumber for a whole house so close there wouldn't be enough scrap left over for kindling.

He checked his list of building materials. "Tomorrow, we'll go to the lumber company in town," he said. "And before long, we'll have us a boat."

But we didn't get to the lumber company the next day. After supper, Mr. Gillem introduced us to Mr. Mulgrove, who offered to teach Daddy about pole and line fishing. He said if they left early, they could get a tow from a shrimp boat to some better fishing spots in the bay and sail back to the harbor when they were ready to sell their catch.

I could tell Daddy was excited. He asked Mr. Mulgrove how he'd rigged a sail to his skiff, and before Daddy went to sleep, materials for a mast had been added to his lumber list. Mama said she had enough quilting scraps to make a sail and would start on one right away.

The next morning around four, the cannery whistle blew, calling the workers in. Mama fixed some breakfast for Daddy, and soon after, he pulled on his worn leather gloves and followed Mr. Mulgrove up one of the seawall trails. At first I worried that the slope might be too steep for Daddy. Then I reminded myself that he'd probably sized up the problem when we first got here. Though there was little he couldn't do, he was smart about his limitations. I watched him through the tent flap, a dark shadow moving up the trail to the narrow maintenance road that ran on top. Mr. Mulgrove's taller figure kept with Daddy's slower pace, and they soon disappeared down the other side, where the boat was docked.

When they were gone, I was too hungry to go back to sleep. I guess Mama didn't like the idea of spending more time in our crowded tent, either. She sat on the storage box outside, staring at the halo of purple light just above the seawall. I slipped out, careful not to wake the kids, and sat down beside her to watch my first sunrise in this place. In the still half-light of morning, I smelled the bay and the salt cedars. I heard a baby whimper, the clunk of pot against stove, the squeak of an outhouse door.

"It'll be September soon," Mama said without looking at me. "You and Jacob need school clothes."

I hadn't given school much thought till now, but Mama was right. August was near half gone. It was hard to imagine what it would be like going to a strange school with kids I didn't know. I tried to picture them sitting next to me in class, brushing against me in halls, staring at me over their noon meal. My stomach fluttered, and I found myself wishing like everything that Wilma were here. I glanced at Dollie's house, black as night, wrapped in all that tar paper. She might not be Wilma, but at least I wouldn't be alone my first day of seventh grade.

The purple halo over the seawall widened, taking on tinges of pink and gold. A rooster crowed—Mr. Caughlin's, I figured, from down the lane. I heard a stirring from inside the tent and knew it wouldn't be long before the kids would be up.

Mama put her hand on my knee. I thought she was going to tell me it was time to start breakfast, but she had something else on her mind.

"There won't be any new material for your school dresses this year, Sadie."

I looked at her, waiting, but I knew what was coming.

"I saved some pretty flour sack prints for you, though."

I was used to Mama making our underthings out of flour sacks, but I'd always gotten store-bought material for my school dresses. I listened to her talk about putting rickrack around the collars and hems and tried to imagine my first day in a strange school wearing a flour-sack dress. I knew better than to complain, but words popped out of me like they had a life of their own.

"But Daddy sold the house, Mama, and we picked cotton. I thought we had enough."

Mama sighed. "We need a boat, Sadie, *and* a house. It might not snow here, but getting through a cold, windy winter in a tent would be hard, especially with a new baby to care for."

She left me sitting on the box and pulled out a pan for oatmeal. I got up to help, but I wasn't hungry anymore.

After the kids were fed and chores were done, we looked through the Montgomery Ward catalog and picked out a new dress style. Mama could copy almost anything, and I felt somewhat better remembering that. Those flour sacks just might turn into something that could pass for store-bought. She measured me and Jacob ever' which-a-way and compared the measurements to some old patterns. We'd grown, and the paper patterns would have to be enlarged. We sorted through her stack of quilting scraps and folded sacks, matching up prints to see what we could make. We had enough for three shirts for Jacob, and three dresses and a new slip for me. Mama looked pleased.

While I pinned pattern pieces to material, I looked for Dollie. I thought for sure she would've popped up beside me by now, prattling on about this and that, wanting to help, but she never showed up.

By early evening, I saw Daddy and Mr. Mulgrove coming back over the seawall. Mr. Mulgrove carried a tow sack slung over his shoulder. Daddy had his tied to his back, dragging in the dirt behind him. Me and the kids ran across the lane to meet them and tormented Daddy with more questions than he could answer. He handed Jacob the bag. "Trout," he said. "Too small to sell."

Jacob looked inside and hollered across the lane. "We're having fish for supper, Mama."

Mama stood by the tent, waiting, her hand shading her eyes. She waved, and Daddy shooed us off with a promise to tell us more about the fishing over supper. He shook Mr. Mulgrove's hand, thanked him, and started across the lane.

Mama met Daddy in the shade of the tent with coffee. But before he took the cup, he pulled money from his pocket and handed it to her. "A dollar and twenty-two cents," I heard him say.

Mama smiled and sat down beside him.

"We can make a living here, Raine," he told her. "It won't be long before we're out of this tent."

I pulled in a deep breath, relieved Daddy was so hopeful. I could wear flour-sack dresses this year if it helped us save money. If we saved enough, maybe we could move away from all these black papered shacks. Maybe Daddy would take us home.

Chapter Seven

THERE MUST'VE BEEN a dozen little fish in Daddy's sack, already gutted. He poured them into Mama's dishpan, and with them tumbled creatures I'd never seen before.

"Will they bite?" Bobby asked.

Daddy shook his head. "They're dead."

Emily pointed to a hard-shelled thing with big pinchers. "What is it?" she whispered.

"I know," said Jacob. "It's a crab. I saw them when I was with Oren. And this is a baby squid." He picked up a pale sea animal with long squiggly-looking legs. "Oren said people fry them up crisp and eat them."

"Not me!" Emily slapped a hand over her mouth and backed away.

Daddy pulled out a shrimp and showed it to Mama. "This is where the big money is," he said. He pinched off the head, peeled away the shell, and laid the shrimp in his palm. We all stared at the clean, white meat.

I finally knew what "heading shrimp" meant. All those people at the cannery were pinching the heads off shrimp and peeling off the tough, papery skin. Daddy did five more and put all six in the dishpan with the fish. "One for each of us," he said. "It's time we tasted for ourselves what all the fuss is about."

I helped Mama scale the fish and wash them. She cut off the heads, added a few gashes to the sides, and rolled them in cornmeal along with the shrimp. The fish browned up nice and tasted good with Mama's biscuits and black-eyed peas, but we all agreed there was something special about fried shrimp.

While we ate, Daddy told us how he caught piggy perch for bait. "Trout love 'em," he said. "They got us some whoppers."

"How big were the trout?" Jacob asked.

Daddy stretched his hands out to show the length. "A few must've been six or seven pounds apiece."

Emily frowned. "But why'd you call the bait piggy perch, Daddy?"

He leaned close and whispered, " 'Cause they make

a sound just like a little pig." He grunted around her neck, and she squealed.

Bobby laughed and hollered, "Me too!"

So Daddy grunted for Bobby, too.

I watched Daddy laughing, still lit up with the adventure of it all, and I couldn't help but wonder if the drought had been an excuse for his coming here. Maybe a life of fishing was what he'd wanted all along.

After supper, a man walking down the road turned onto our lane. He tipped his hat, nodded at Daddy, then smiled when he saw me and Mama washing up supper dishes. I smiled back, even though his clothes were dusty and his grayish hair too long.

Something about him made my insides ache, but I couldn't put my finger on what exactly. Could've been the tired slope of his thin shoulders. Or maybe it was the slow rise and fall of his chest that said life was just too painful to keep breathing for. He walked up to Mama, his sweat-stained hat in his hands, and I saw a look in his eyes—a kind of blue bewilderment that hinted at loss so deep, my heart grieved for him.

"Evening, ma'am," he said.

Mama nodded, and his blue-eyed gaze dropped to the ground.

"I haven't eaten since yesterday, and I was wondering if you had a little something you could spare?"

Mama nodded again. She never turned anyone away hungry. The fish and beans were gone, but she pulled a cup towel from the two biscuits we hadn't finished. She spread grape jelly through the middles and held them out. "Good luck to you," she said.

The man's head bobbed as he took the bread. "Thank you kindly, ma'am. Blessings to you."

I watched him head back to the road, a big bite already gone from one of the biscuits. It made me wish I could call him back like a stray pup and take care of him. I slipped to the ground beside Daddy. "Where do you reckon he'll sleep tonight?" I whispered.

Daddy sat quiet, his eyes full like he'd seen farther than he'd wanted. He stared toward the seawall till the man disappeared over the top. "These are hard times, Babygirl," he said. "Wouldn't hurt to mention him in your prayers tonight."

I nodded, and Daddy added, "Wouldn't hurt to count your blessings, either."

The next morning, I helped with breakfast while Mama got ready to go to town with Daddy. They'd

< 55 >

be picking out lumber for the new boat today, and I'd be watching the kids. Mama covered the beans she'd soaked overnight with fresh water, added salt and pepper and a spoonful of lard, and put them on to cook.

"Watch this pot now, Sadie," she told me. "Keep it at a simmer and don't let those beans cook dry."

"Yes, ma'am."

After they left and my chores were done, I sat down to add to Wilma's letter. It was looking fat as a diary, and I hoped it wouldn't take two stamps. I decided I'd better write smaller. I'd already told her about our trip to Texas, about seeing the ocean and picking cotton. And I told her about the Gillems, too.

I glanced at the house next door and remembered that I hadn't seen Dollie at all yesterday. I wondered if she was sick. I left Emily and Bobby drawing pictures on a sheet of my notebook paper and knocked on Mrs. Gillem's door. She came to the screen, holding a fan in one hand and Caleb in the other. "Hi, Sadie," she said. "Whatcha need this hot morning?"

"Morning, Mrs. Gillem. I was wondering if Dollie was sick or something. I didn't see her around yesterday."

"Oh, she's fine," Mrs. Gillem said between swipes of her fan. "It's Lou Ann Waller who's sick. Dollie's helping today with the kids so Mrs. Waller can work, but tomorrow morning, she'll be at the cannery with her papa." Her fan never missed a beat. "I'll tell her you asked after her when she gets in tonight."

I nodded, not at all sure I wanted Dollie to know that, but I thanked Mrs. Gillem just the same and went back to the kids.

Mama and Daddy didn't get back till almost noon. Mama carried a paper sack in her arms, tender as a baby, and Daddy hollered at Jacob to fetch the groceries from the backseat. I unpacked sacks of flour, sugar, and beans, then tins of coffee and lard, and put them away in our storage box. Mama set her package beside the stove and checked the simmering pot.

"What's in the sack, Mama?" I asked.

"Light bread and butter," she said.

There were grins all around. We loved the cloud-soft store-bought bread, and it had been a long time since we'd had butter on the table.

Later, when we'd had our fill of beans and the last slice of bread was gone, a lumber truck turned onto our lane and rumbled to a stop. A man unloaded a box of nails, paint, and long, sweet-smelling boards beside our tent. Before the truck was out of sight, Daddy was gathering his tools.

The first thing he did was build legs on the storage box so Mama could keep out the ants and roaches.

< 57 >

He set the legs in empty coffee tins and filled them with water.

"There won't be any more roaches nibbling in *that* box." He winked at us. "Unless the good Lord taught 'em to swim last night."

All afternoon I helped Mama with the kids while she sewed together flour-sack pieces. And all afternoon I watched Daddy work on his boat.

Toward evening, we saw Mr. Caughlin walking to town with his big yellow dog. He stopped to say hello and made old River grin for us. The dog nuzzled my hand and grinned again. Bobby giggled, but Emily wanted to know what River was so happy about.

"Just pleased to meet new folks," Mr. Caughlin said.

He waved good-bye and headed down the road. River trotted close at his heels, his tongue hanging from the side of his mouth.

Seeing that dog, feeling his warm breath on my hand, made me miss our old Ruby something fierce. She was always waiting for me when I came home from school, tail wagging so hard she had trouble keeping her hind legs on the ground. It'd be hard to find another dog as good as she was.

Before supper, a neighbor from across the lane introduced himself to Daddy. He said his name was

Harley Winslow, but I didn't get to hear more than that 'cause Mama put her sewing away and called me to help with supper. Mr. Winslow talked awhile, then Daddy followed the man back to his house. I watched Daddy make his way around the ragged tar-papered walls and point to the roof before he went inside. I figured Mr. Winslow must've heard what a good carpenter Daddy was and asked his help in fixing up the place.

Later, Daddy came back alone. I saw him talking to Mama, their faces serious like they were pondering something important. When we were through eating, Mama crossed the lane with Daddy, leaving me and Jacob to clean up. She walked past the worn-out old table sitting under Mr. Winslow's chinaberry tree and straight to the outhouse. After a quick look inside, she joined the men.

"What do you think's going on?" I asked Jacob.

He shrugged. "Maybe Mr. Winslow's sick and needs help."

I shook my head. "He didn't look sick."

"Maybe he's gonna pay Daddy to fix up his house."

"Maybe. But why would he pay for work he could do himself?"

Jacob shrugged.

Shortly after Mama and Daddy got back, I saw

Mr. Winslow head toward the main road. He had a carpetbag in his hand. He smiled our way and waved, and Daddy waved back.

"Where's Mr. Winslow going?" Jacob asked.

"He's leaving to live with his daughter in town."

Something in Daddy's voice set off a flutter in my belly. I looked at him, uneasy, and waited.

"Mr. Winslow won't be needing his house anymore. He made us a good offer, so I bought it."

His words hit me like a slap. I stared at him. He was smiling. Mama smiled, too, like all this was just fine with her. I jerked around to look across the lane, and my head pounded. The house sat in the corner of the seawall by the road, black and ugly. Torn tar paper curled from the sides and corners.

"Can we go see it?" Jacob asked.

"Please, Daddy," Emily begged.

Daddy nodded.

Mama took my hand and led me across the lane. She said something about the house needing a little fixing, but that in time we'd make it nice. I stepped inside the tiny one-room house onto a hard-packed dirt floor, and the tightness in my head spread to my throat. I could still hear Mama talking behind me, but I couldn't answer.

A patchwork of water-stained cardboard covered the walls and ceiling. In the corner sat an icebox—

door open, empty. And above it, plates and bowls rested on shelves. A little worktable held an oven and camp stove, and on the burners sat a black pot and skillet, waiting for the next meal.

I heard Mama talking again, planning. New floor, she said. Beds.

I felt numb.

A hammock piled with old quilts hung from the ceiling, and under it sat an old rocking chair with a broken arm. In another corner stood a potbelly stove and a table with benches. But it was nothing like Daddy's table.

Mama kept talking behind me like this was a real house. More shelves, a new roll of screening for the windows. I looked at the square openings covered with torn and rusted mesh. They weren't real windows at all. They had no glass, just wooden covers that had to be propped open with a stick.

I shook off the numbness and backed out the door. I started across the lane, but when I saw Daddy waiting, I turned and ran to the top of the seawall. I felt like running all the way back to Missouri. To a real house. My house. A house with walls and floors and a front porch.

I wanted to go home.

I crawled into the cedars beside the narrow road. I needed time to sort things out. I knew it was a sin to hold this kind of poison in my heart, but my thoughts were a jumble of bitterness and my heart wouldn't listen. It felt stone cold and empty. I couldn't even cry.

I looked toward the heavens, soft with evening color. "I need help," I whispered.

I waited. The colors deepened.

I watched ants marching back to their dens, spiders spinning webs, doodlebugs digging funnels in the sand. They all had homes.

I waited some more, but no angels swept down to help me. No heavenly words of wisdom rang in my ears.

The sun slipped out of sight, and my hiding place grew dim. I couldn't stay any longer or Mama and Daddy would be mad.

I pushed myself up and startled a sparrow. It flew down the road and took up a new roost near a large cardboard box nestled in the cedars. Something stirred, and it flew again. I looked closer and recognized the man Mama had fed last night asleep inside the box. He shifted and pulled his knees up closer to his chest.

I stared at him a long time, watching him sleep, wondering if he was hungry, wondering what sorrowful thing had led him to make a cardboard box his home. I thought about our tar-paper shack and remembered the relief on Daddy's face when he told us about it. And I felt shame.

It was then the tears rolled out of me—silent, like rain down a windowpane.

When I got back, the kids were chasing lightning bugs, giggling over their pickle jar of blinking lights. Mama and Daddy didn't say a word to me. I didn't blame them. Instead of counting my blessings like Daddy asked me to do, I'd been feeding my bitterness.

Mama stood by the storage box, picking over beans for tomorrow by lamplight. "I'll wash those for you, Mama," I said.

She gave me a curious look, then handed me the pot. While I washed the beans, I saw Dollie coming down the lane. She waved, but I ducked my head and pretended I hadn't seen her. I couldn't bear the thought of being cornered with stories about her day of babysitting. Not tonight. She slipped through her screen door and let me be.

I left the beans soaking in fresh water for tomorrow and found Mama again. She sat by Daddy outside the tent, the last rays of sunset shimmering in her dark hair. I sat beside her and watched Daddy shake tobacco onto a square of white paper. He pulled the drawstring bag closed with his teeth and rolled a cigarette.

I glanced across the lane. Our new house huddled in the corner of the seawall, almost swallowed up by the dark. It looked as sad and lost as the man sleeping in the cardboard box had.

"Will you be working on the house tomorrow, Mama?" I asked.

When she didn't answer right away, I was afraid she was too mad at me to speak. But she finally nodded and said, "We will."

"Can I help?" I asked, my breath in a knot.

This time, the answer came quicker. "You can," she said.

I let the tangled air out real slow. Tomorrow would be different. I'd see to it.

Chapter Eight

I WOKE with the cannery whistle the next day, dreaming of the man on the seawall. I'd taken to thinking of him as Mr. Sparrow, since it was the bird that led me to see him sleeping. In a way, we were alike, this man and me—him with his cardboard house and me with my tar-paper one. He probably had a real house once, too, just like me. But asleep or awake, I kept seeing his sad blue eyes. I wondered if he was curled up in his box right now, awake and hungry, waiting for the sun to rise. Then I worried that sorrow might've sunk so deep in his heart, he wouldn't care if the sun rose ever again. That last notion crawled in and out of my thoughts, dark as death's door, till I couldn't bear thinking of him anymore.

I glanced out the tent flap and saw black shadows moving against the moonlit sky. Workers picked their way up a dozen seawall trails, pulled toward the cannery like they were under a spell. I figured Dollie had to be one of them and tried to spot her matchstick body and bushy curls, but it was still too dark. I gave up and slipped out to the Gillems' outhouse. When I got back, Mama was up and making biscuits. I glanced at her, wondering if she was mad at me still. She didn't look it, but I couldn't be sure.

No matter how hard I tried, Mr. Sparrow managed to stay at the edge of my thoughts. It was like he was watching me. Seeing me reach for a biscuit. Heap fig preserves into the soft, steaming middle. Like he could see every bite.

After breakfast, Mama poured the last of our water into her iron pot to wash Mr. Winslow's old quilts. She sent Jacob off to fill the water buckets and left me to clean up the breakfast dishes. She and Daddy had to make one more trip to town. "The last," Mama said, " 'cause money can't be wasted on gasoline till we have fish to sell."

Daddy said he'd mail my letter if I had it ready. I made out the envelope in a hurry, scribbling my name and "General Delivery, Aransas Pass, Texas," in the upper left corner. Now Wilma would be able to write me, too. I couldn't wait to hear back from her.

As soon as Mama and Daddy drove away, I grabbed our leftover biscuits for Mr. Sparrow, talked Jacob into watching the kids, and hurried up the seawall. My heart thudded, and my thoughts scampered like field mice. I was fearful he wouldn't be there. And fearful he would.

When I reached the top, I peeked around the cedars and down the narrow road. The box sat wedged between the tree limbs, but it was upside down. Mr. Sparrow was nowhere around. I stood there holding the biscuits, staring at the box, wondering what was underneath. Could be it was nothing. Could be he'd moved on. But my need to know pulled hard at me.

I eased closer. The brown box, dew-damp and smelly, had once held a new radio. Even upside down, I could read the letters "RCA." It was foolish to think of looking underneath, but I knelt at the road's edge, anyway, and wiggled my fingers under the corner.

I lifted the end and saw a change of clothes and a dented tin box. The tin must've held Christmas sweets once. Santa's merry eyes and rosy cheeks showed through the rust. I glanced around to make sure no one was looking and pulled off the lid.

Inside, I found a small piece of pan bread wrapped in brown paper. I lifted it gently, and beneath lay a dozen tiny birds carved from cedar—gulls, sparrows, doves, blue herons—all of them with finely etched feathers. A pelican, his body half-trapped in a rough cedar block, was the only one not finished.

In the bottom of the tin, beyond the beaks and wings, I saw a photograph. From between the heron's legs, Mr. Sparrow's paper eyes gazed up at me. I slid the picture out for a closer look. He appeared much younger in his tailored suit and striped tie. He stood beside a pretty lady holding a baby, and four children, shiny clean in their white collars and buttoned shoes, stood gathered in front of them. Behind them loomed a two-story house with a wraparound porch—a big house with shutters and fancy trim and rosebushes. Grand as old Mr. Sanderson's place back home.

What kind of misery could've separated him from a home and family like this? I wondered. I stared at the picture till some stray oyster shell from the road cut into my knees and brought me to my senses. What if Mr. Sparrow came back? Tossing nervous glances down the trail, I returned the photo and pan bread. Then, remembering my biscuits, I shoved them into the tin, too. I pushed it all back under the box and ran back to camp.

My heart pounded so hard, I barely noticed Jacob's scowls.

< 68 >

"What were you doing up there on that seawall?" he asked.

"Nothing, Jacob. Better get that water now, or Mama will be mad." I busied myself with the dirty dishes and listened for the sound of his leaving. He must've decided to let me be 'cause I heard the handles squeak on the metal buckets. I turned to see him headed toward the road, a bucket swinging from each hand.

I went back to cleaning up, all the while thinking about Mr. Sparrow's life frozen in that photograph. I couldn't fathom how a man who once had so much could be sleeping on the seawall in a cardboard box. Where was his family?

Jacob had just poured the last bucket of water into the rinse tub when Mama and Daddy got back. Mama put me to washing Mr. Winslow's quilts, so I let my pondering about Mr. Sparrow go. I watched Jacob, instead, unloading tar paper and cardboard from the car. I didn't see any boards or screening. Like gasoline, I figured the new floor and windows would have to wait, too.

Daddy began work on his boat while me and Mama finished the laundry. "Tonight," she said, "we'll have extra quilts to sleep on till Daddy can build us some beds."

That sounded good to me. I was tired of sleeping with nothing but a blanket and an old wagon sheet between me and the hard ground.

When the clean quilts were hanging on the line, me and Jacob rolled the tar paper across the lane to the house. Davis and Oren must've seen what we were doing 'cause they brought their daddy's ladder over for us. I watched Davis jogging across the lane, balancing the ladder with ease. He was big for thirteen and had escaped all the curly red hair Dollie and Oren inherited. Davis's hair was shiny brown like his mama's with only a curl here and there to link him to the Gillem clan.

"No need for you and Sadie to be climbing up on that roof, Mrs. Wynn," he said. "I'd be happy to help."

"Don't you have to work today, Davis?" Mama asked.

"Not today." He swelled with importance. "Our boat's got a problem, so the crew's killing time till it's fixed."

Mama thanked him, but it was me that got his smile. I ducked my head, determined not to blush again, but I felt my cheeks color up just the same. I kicked the roll of tar paper closer to the house.

We set to work papering. Me and Mama measured and cut, Jacob and Oren held it in place, and

Davis nailed it. The black tar heated up quick under the sun, and the still morning reeked of it.

It was clear the Gillem boys had done this kind of work before. Sweat dripped off their noses, but Davis didn't miss a beat with the hammer till I ran across the lane to check on the simmering beans. I added more water to the pot and caught him watching me with his green eyes. He pretended to be wiping his face with his shirttail, but I knew what he was doing. It got me flustered, just like he knew it would, and that got me mad. Davis needed a lesson. He needed to know what a red face felt like.

I went back to cutting tar paper and managed to avoid more looks. When the work was done, Davis climbed down from the roof, hooked an arm through a rung on the ladder, and hoisted it over his shoulder. "That oughta do it, Mrs. Wynn."

Mama smiled her thanks and wiped her face with the tail of her apron.

"If we can do anything else, just holler," Davis said. He looked straight at me and grinned wider than Mr. Caughlin's dog. "Anytime," he said.

This time I was ready for him. I clamped my jaw tight and stared at him through half-closed eyes, cold and hard. There was no way he was going to make me blush again.

Puzzlement crept into his eyes and settled heavy across his brow. The cocky look on his face drained away. He glanced at his feet, turned, and shuffled off.

I smiled to myself while I gathered up our tools. He deserved every bit of the discomfort he got after the way he'd embarrassed me with his flirty ways. I turned to carry the tools back to Daddy's box and glimpsed Davis hanging the ladder on the side of his house. He sat on the front step with a busted bait box between his feet and reached for his hammer, but he never looked my way.

"Good," I whispered to myself. "That's exactly what I wanted—to be left alone."

I got a long drink of water for me and the kids, ladled more into a cup for Mama, and headed back across the lane.

I stole another look at Davis before I got to the house. I knew he must've seen me 'cause he ducked his head fast and slumped over his work.

I'd embarrassed him, all right. I felt an uneasy sinking in my belly, but I pulled in a deep breath and the uncomfortable feeling passed. Could've been the water, I decided finally, and hurried in to Mama.

With the house safe from rain, we started on the inside. Mama had us prop open all the windows and haul everything but the potbelly stove out for

< 72 >

scrubbing. Emily and Bobby were more hindrance than help, but we waited patiently while they grunted and pushed a bench through the door. When the house was bare, we pulled down the worst of the stained cardboard and nailed up new pieces. I never did like the smell of cardboard and figured poor Mr. Sparrow must feel the same by now.

Nothing was safe from Mama's lye soap, not even the broken rocker or the outhouse seat. I didn't know what was worse, the smelly old tar paper or those big bars of soap that turned my hands red as vine-ripe tomatoes. Eager to make up for my selfishness, I didn't complain, though.

While Emily and Bobby dried everything off with rags, me and Jacob made a dozen trips to our campsite and back again, dragging all our belongings to the house. The only things left sitting in the hot sun were Daddy and his boat lumber. That's when Jacob got the idea that our tent could be used for shade. "Like a porch," he said. I moved aside the weathered table that Mr. Winslow had left and helped stretch the tent from the chinaberry tree to the side of the house. I didn't see how Jacob could compare the tent shade to a real porch. It was just a lean-to, but still, I hoped Mama might let us sleep there in the open air.

She had other plans, though. She wanted to do the

< 73 >

cooking outside to keep from heating up the house. So the camp stove and oven went under the new lean-to, along with the storage box.

With the kitchen set up, Mama went back inside and swept the dirt floor so clean it surprised even me. Then we moved everything in but the old rocker and arranged it the way she wanted—the wobbly table near the front by the wood stove and the wagon sheet laid in the rear with fresh quilts folded on top.

I breathed in the clean scent of soap, then caught a different smell. The house was sweet, but we weren't. Emily and Bobby grinned at me from behind streaks of sweaty grime, making me glad I couldn't see my own face. I took them outside, wet a rag, and heard hammering coming from the house. I hurried to wash us all, curious to see what Mama was doing.

I sent Emily and Bobby off to play, and when I stepped back inside I saw Mama's best quilt hanging on the wall. The double wedding ring pattern splashed color across the dull cardboard as pretty as any wallpaper or fancy painting.

I helped her hang Daddy's cherry-brown fiddle on the right side of the door and her oval-framed picture of Grandma and Grandpa on the other. The photograph and a rose-patterned teapot were all we had left of them. We set the teapot on the topmost shelf and lined up Daddy's books on the lower ones.

When I didn't think she could do any more, Mama spread her ivory crocheted cloth over the rickety table, the same cloth that had sat on Daddy's shiny drop-leaf table back home. For a moment, I glimpsed loss in Mama's eyes. I figured she missed Daddy's beautiful table same as I did. But just as quickly as the sadness came, it was gone. She took my hand, stood back, and looked at the house.

It was changed. Mama had managed to turn Mr. Winslow's ugly black box into something he'd probably never recognize. She'd made it ours.

Mama drew a deep breath and wiped her red hands against her apron.

"Sit down, Mama," I said. She looked hot and tired. "I'll get you some water."

When I got back she was settled at the table, her belly pushing against the splintered edge. Our December baby had been growing. "A Christmas gift," Mama had called it when she told us about the little one coming. "Like baby Jesus?" Emily had asked.

Mama sipped at her water and inspected the room like I'd seen her do a hundred times already. I couldn't imagine what she was thinking. I figured it had to be worrisome, though, 'cause the crease between her eyes deepened. I felt again the shame that comes from seeing your own selfishness, and hoped it wasn't me that made her worry so. I couldn't change yesterday, but

I'd done my best to make today better. It felt good, but I wanted Mama to feel good, too.

"You made the house look real nice, Mama," I said, still somewhat surprised I really meant it.

She rested her arms on the table, and when she smiled at me, I knew I'd been forgiven.

Chapter Nine

THE SEAWALL BLOCKED the bay breezes, allowing the evening sun to heat up the house something terrible. Mama looked so tuckered out, me and Jacob carried a bench out for her and set it under the lean-to near the chinaberry tree. While she rested her back against the tree trunk, I helped Jacob move Daddy's boat lumber closer to the house—all of it but the pieces out by the ditch.

It hadn't rained in a while, according to Mr. Gillem, but the ditch was full of water just the same. "Mostly tidewater," Daddy said. "Salty." He poked a stick into the brackish water to check the depth, then slid the boards in. I knew what he was doing. I'd seen him soak short pieces of staircase railing in a rain barrel once. The boat's sides would have to curve toward a pointed bow, and soaking would let the wood bend without splitting.

Jacob carried the tools while Daddy made his way across the lane to our new house. He hadn't seen what we'd done to the inside yet, but he already had a big grin on his face. He poked his head through the door, took a quick look, and tickled Emily's ribs. "You couldn't have done all this work by yourselves," he said. "Must've been fairies."

"Uh-uh," Bobby said. "We did it. We did it all." He sidled up to Daddy, waiting for his turn to be tickled, and was quickly obliged.

Daddy winked at me and tossed Mama a look—one I'd seen before, a look I knew was meant for just her. Mama always smiled back like they shared some great secret.

I got up to help Mama with supper and saw Dollie coming down the seawall trail. She caught sight of us sitting beside the house and shot us a silly grin.

"I can't believe what I'm seeing," she said. "Can I look inside, Mrs. Wynn?"

Mama nodded, and Dollie leaned through the doorway, her head swiveling back and forth. "It's plumb amazing. Mr. Winslow never had this place looking so nice." She poked me in the ribs. "It's so clean. How'd you get it done so fast?"

"Davis and Oren were a big help this morning with the tar paper," Mama said.

Dollie nodded. "I'm sorry I wasn't here to help, too, but I'm glad you're going to stay."

Stay? The word hit my belly like a fist. We weren't going to stay. We'd be going home as soon as things were better in Missouri. I stared hard at Dollie, then glanced at Daddy. He hadn't seen my worry at all. He was more interested in what Dollie had been up to.

"I've been helping Lou Ann Waller watch her brothers and sisters," Dollie said. "But today I worked with Papa at the cannery, peeling shrimp." Her usual grin stretched extra wide. "Made fifteen cents today."

"Fifteen cents?" I blinked hard while the amount sunk in, then did some quick figuring. Six days' pay would be almost a dollar.

Dollie nodded. "Five cents a bucket. They had an extra-good catch, so I got to peel three buckets this morning instead of the usual two." She glanced at her red fingers. "Going again tomorrow."

"Daddy, can I go with her?" I asked.

Mama frowned, and I knew that meant trouble. If she objected, Daddy might not ever let me go.

"Lots of kids work there," I blurted. "Even Oren, and he's only ten."

Jacob brightened at the mention of Oren's name. "Can I go, too, Daddy?" he asked.

Daddy shook his head. "I need you to help with the boat."

Jacob slumped onto the bench, and my hopes sank, too.

"Will your papa be taking you tomorrow?" Mama asked.

Dollie nodded. "It's the only way he'll let me go."

I saw uncertainty in Mama's eyes, but not in Daddy's. I held my breath.

"You can go," he said finally, "but only if Mr. Gillem doesn't mind."

"Papa won't mind," Dollie said. "I'm sure of it."

I felt light-headed. "What time?" I asked.

Dollie shrugged. "Papa's up and ready to go before the four o'clock whistle."

"I'll be ready," I said.

Dollie nodded, said her good-byes, and took off across the lane.

After supper, Mama sat down with her sewing. I wound the clock and set it for three-thirty, then tried to go to sleep. I could hardly believe I had a real job. Tomorrow I'd be working at the Rice Cannery. I lay there, listening to the minutes tick away, wondering how many days a week Mr. Gillem worked. I hoped he'd let me go with him as often as I wanted. Even after school started, I might work a few hours before the bell.

I smiled. It was a good plan. For the first time, I felt like I had a hand in my own fate. I could help Mama and Daddy save money. Things were bound to get better in Missouri, and when they did, I'd be ready. I'd save enough to get us back home. I might even save enough to get Wilma and her family back home, too. I fell asleep wondering how long it took to head and peel a bucket of shrimp.

When Dollie and Mr. Gillem came for me the next morning, I was outside waiting. I could hardly see them crossing the lane in the dark, but I could tell they weren't alone.

"Davis's boat is still in dock," Dollie whispered, "so he'll be working with us today."

I nodded to him, but I guess he didn't see me. Without a word, he turned toward the seawall trail.

I followed them up, thankful they knew their way. Once on top, I squinted, thinking I might make out a corner of Mr. Sparrow's box. But even with a quarter moon, the morning was still too black.

Giving up, I turned toward the harbor and sucked in a breath. I'd never seen the bay at night, and the sight rooted me to the spot. Starlight glittered across the calm black water like a million lightning bugs.

And right through the middle, the quarter moon's reflection drifted serene as one of heaven's angels. It was so beautiful, I hardly remembered to breathe.

"What are you doing?" Dollie whispered, annoyed at my dallying. She grabbed my hand and jerked me down to the harbor, where we joined a string of shadowy figures. We followed them to the end of the road and crossed a short bridge to a large tin building hunched over the water. When the four o'clock whistle blew, the double wooden doors swung open and light spilled across us. I blinked in the brightness and pushed through the doorway with the rest of the workers.

Once inside the cannery, I smelled fresh shrimp. I spotted them in a rear corner beside more open doorways—a huge pile, iced down in boarded pens, waiting to be headed and peeled. Men shoveled the white creatures into wire baskets and dumped them, crushed ice and all, onto long tables where workers already stood along each side. But I didn't see any canning going on.

Dollie tugged at my dress and pointed toward a stack of buckets. "Hurry," she said, "or we won't get a place."

I grabbed my bucket and bellied up to a table between Dollie and Mr. Gillem. Davis walked around to the other side and squeezed in between Mrs. Pickens and Mr. Caughlin. "If this is a cannery," I whispered to Dollie, "why isn't anyone canning?"

"The real canning is done at a place closer to town," she said. "Our job is to get the shrimp ready."

The tables filled up fast. I looked back at the door and saw people being turned away. I remembered Daddy saying, "These are hard times, Babygirl," and I wondered if the whole world was like this—too many people and not enough jobs.

Mr. Gillem pulled something from his pocket. "Let me see your hands, Sadie."

I held out my hands, and he rubbed my fingers with a chunk of alum.

"This'll toughen you up a bit," he said. He passed the alum on to Dollie. "Just watch, and do what we do."

In the middle of the table, piped water ran down a long trough and into a hole in the floor. I saw it splash into the bay below, but before I could ask Dollie about it, a man dumped shrimp onto our table and everyone started working.

Mr. Gillem grabbed a shrimp, pinched off the head, and peeled it so fast I hardly saw his fingers move. He tossed the peelings into the trough and grabbed another shrimp. The water washed the peelings to the end of the trough, where they disappeared with others, over the edge and into the bay. Green water boiled with hungry catfish as more peelings hit the surface.

Simple enough, I thought, but I needed a better look at how that papery skin came off. I turned to Dollie. She showed me where to peel first, stripped the meat clean, then held it up for me to see.

I nodded and picked up my first shrimp. It was icy cold. I didn't much care for pinching off the head, but I didn't do too badly. When I had it peeled, I held it up for her approval.

Dollie grinned. "Good work. Now get another one. You've got a long way to go before you fill that bucket, and you won't get a whole nickel unless it's brimming full."

I looked across the table. Davis already had a small pile of clean shrimp in front of him, and so did Mr. Gillem.

I tossed my peelings into the trough and looked to see how much Dollie had done. I counted five, and she was reaching for another. I'd have to work a lot faster if I hoped to make any money.

I set my mind to building up speed, but it got harder and harder to avoid the sharp shrimp horns. They poked and stabbed into me no matter how careful I was. After a bad gouging, I flinched and caught Davis looking at me. He ducked his head quick, but he needn't have. With the cockiness gone, his watching didn't bother me like it did before.

While I worked, Dollie babbled on and on like she always did. After a while, I guess her daddy had as much of it as he could stand, 'cause he shot her a hard look. She got quiet, then—something I hadn't seen before now. But I was soon wishing I had the old Dollie back chattering at my elbow to help pass the time.

I worked steady, but Dollie filled her bucket twice before my cleaned shrimp finally reached the rim. Davis finished three buckets, and Mr. Gillem, four. I glanced toward the far corner. The shrimp bin was empty.

Some workers had already left the building, and others had pushed to the front to turn in their buckets. A man who looked a lot like Mr. Sparrow collected his pay and disappeared through the door. For a minute, I wanted to run after him, to find out for sure, but Davis motioned at my bucket, reminding me to finish up. I hoped the man I'd seen was Mr. Sparrow. Working men could feed themselves.

I made sure the bucket was rounded full and stood in line for my pay. The line moved, and soon I had a fat nickel clutched in my hand. I thanked Mr. Gillem for letting me go with him, and we headed home.

Davis's behavior had improved toward me, but not toward Dollie. Money jingling in his pocket must've put him in a feisty mood, 'cause he teased his sister shamefully on the way home, chanting "Dollie-Polliwog" till she hollered, "Papa!" in exasperation.

With Mr. Sparrow on my mind, I kept quiet most of the way. If I'd truly seen him, he might've seen me, too. I wondered if he remembered me from that first day outside our tent. I wondered, too, what went through his mind when he found my biscuits in his tin.

My chest pounded even before we reached the sea-wall trail. Once on top, I glanced down the narrow road. The box was still there, but Mr. Sparrow wasn't. Disappointment anchored me to the spot, and I ended up letting the Gillems disappear down the other side of the wall without me. That's when Mr. Sparrow stood and stepped from behind his box.

He looked straight at me.

I sucked in a quick breath and stared back.

He smiled and nodded.

I felt my face color up and rushed off down the trail. But even before I reached the house, I was mad at myself. He probably just wanted to thank me for the biscuits, and I'd bolted like a witless child.

I jumped through our open doorway and startled Mama. She frowned and wrinkled her nose. "Goodness," she said. "Look at you, Sadie."

The front of my dress was wet and smelly. I brushed at it, forgetting all about Mr. Sparrow, and showed Mama my nickel. But it wasn't the money she saw; it was my swollen hands.

She shook her head, dragged me to the washbowl, and bathed every cut on my red hands. Then she rubbed them with salve to ease the soreness. "Better stay home a few days," she said. "Let these hands heal a bit."

"But I have to go, Mama." I put my nickel in an empty mason jar and held it up for her to see. "This is a real job."

She sighed and set my jar on the shelf by her rose-patterned teapot. "You've got a lot of your daddy in you, Sadie."

I sighed, too, but with relief. As long as she didn't say no, I could go again tomorrow.

Dollie knocked at the open door and stuck her head in. "Forgot to tell you, Sadie. *The Lone Ranger* is on tonight. A bunch of us kids are gonna sit outside the Haukes' place and listen to their radio. Wanna come?"

I glanced at Mama. "Is it okay?"

She looked puzzled, like there had to be something wrong with our listening to someone's radio without them knowing, even if we sat off a ways in the salt grass to do it. But in the end, she couldn't figure out why that would be, so she finally agreed. "But don't you bother the Haukes none," she cautioned.

Later that night, me and Jacob gathered in the lane under the stars with a dozen kids from the neighborhood. Davis was there, too, his face shining at the edge of Mrs. Hauke's electric light. When the Lone Ranger hollered, "Hi-yo Silver! Away!" Davis smiled at me—not the arrogant grin from before, but one that seemed to say he'd met his match and didn't mind at all. For the first time since meeting him, I wanted to smile back. I kinda liked this new Davis.

Over the next few days, I thought a lot about what Mama had said. Being like Daddy would've been a fine thing to hear before we moved, but now, I didn't know. He'd been stubborn in bringing us to this place, changing our way of life so we didn't even recognize it anymore. Stubborn and . . . well . . . selfish. But I had to admit I had been, too. I hadn't wanted to live in this one-room house with no floors, and Mama knew it. Maybe that's what she meant when she said I was like Daddy. Maybe selfishness was all Mama saw in me.

Chapter Ten

DAVIS DIDN'T COME with us again to the cannery after that first day. The *Nancy Sue* was finally seaworthy, and by next morning he was out shrimping. I was surprised to find I missed him.

After four days, I still hadn't managed to fill more than a bucket before the shrimp bin was empty. I had twenty cents saved. It was disappointing, but I didn't complain. Even a nickel a day moved me closer to my goal.

Mama spent most of her time sewing, and Daddy spent his working on the boat. But a few times I found him off down the lane when I got back from the cannery, showing a neighbor some carpentry trick or helping Mr. Gillem repair his truck.

Daddy made good on his promise to Mama, too, giving us a Bible verse to ponder every night before we went to sleep. That was fine, but I missed the stories he used to read to us. I had begun to think the move had ended all that, but one evening, he had me fetch his copy of *The Adventures of Tom Sawyer* and promised to read some every night.

On my fifth day at the cannery, I doubled my efforts, determined to do better, and managed to peel a bucket and a half. I added seven cents to my jar that day. That was also the day I came home to find Mama rocking in her newly repaired rocking chair and Daddy's skiff sitting upside down on scrap lumber, the last coat of gray paint drying in the sun.

That evening Mama bought fresh cucumbers from a man going door to door. Someone was always selling homegrown tomatoes or okra or corn. When it came time for supper, I noticed something festive in the way Mama sliced cucumber and sweet onion into vinegar and made corn bread to go with her beans. I figured she must be happy the boat was finished. Daddy must've been, too, 'cause after supper, he sent Jacob for the fiddle.

While Daddy tuned up, Emily and Bobby chased and giggled, too excited to sit still, but they were careful not to wander off very far. Mama fetched her sewing box and sat outside under the chinaberry tree to work on Daddy's sail.

We waited while he plucked at his fiddle. He tightened and loosened strings, drew his bow across them, and then did it all over again. The sounds vibrated inside me, welcome as the rumble of thunder over parched land, and finally, they slid into something I could recognize.

"Wildwood Flower" spilled from Daddy's fiddle, and a sweet sadness welled up inside me as I remembered the way Wilma had loved to hear Daddy play. But even I couldn't stay sad the way Daddy's fiddling sounded tonight. His music filled our shady lean-to and struck out over the neighborhood. I pictured it curling like vines through windows and doorways, turning heads, sparking smiles, and making feet twitch.

Before long, Daddy's fiddle drew neighbors. I saw the Gillems and the Mulgroves, Mr. Caughlin and the Pickens family coming down the lane. Mr. and Mrs. Waller came, too, with Lou Ann and the kids. I even saw Mr. and Mrs. Hauke. Like cats to a fish house, people ambled up to our lean-to and gathered round. They tapped their feet and clapped their hands, and sometimes they sang along.

"How about 'Cotton-Eyed Joe'?" Mr. Gillem asked.

"I'd like to hear 'Under the Double Eagle,'" called Mrs. Waller.

Five-year-old Willa Dean shouted, "Play 'Jingle Bells,' please!"

Everyone laughed, but Daddy played them all and more—waltzes, two-steps, ballads, and a few he wrote himself. He even played "Jingle Bells." Then he asked Mama to sing "Ain't We Crazy." She laughed and refused, but it caused such a clamor, she finally gave in.

Mama's voice rang clear and sweet, but what I loved most was how her own laughter bubbled through the words. She couldn't help it any more than I could've. It was the silliest song I'd ever heard. When she got to the line about the barefoot boy with shoes on, Mr. Gillem slapped his legs and laughed so hard I thought he'd bust a thighbone. But even with all the guffaws around her, Mama never missed a beat. She sang the last two verses, and by the time she got to the chorus, Mr. Gillem had joined in. "Ain't we crazy," they sang. "Ain't we crazy. We're gonna sing this song all night today."

Mama tried to quit then, but everyone wanted more. On the second go-round, voices chimed in left and right till I figured the whole bayfront must've heard us. People walking home from the harbor stopped to listen, and some sat right there at the edge of the road, singing along. One of them pushed past me, stinking of beer, and tried to get Mrs. Waller to dance with him. Mr. Mulgrove and Mr. Gillem quietly pulled him away and sent him packing.

When it got late, Daddy put his fiddle aside and everyone said their good-nights—all but a handful of men who stood out by the boat. Leaning forward, Daddy put a hand on the ground, swung his body off the bench, and went to join them.

"Fine-looking boat you got here, John," Mr. Mulgrove said.

Mr. Waller nodded and ran a hand over the curved bow. "Ain't seen workmanship like this in a long time."

Mr. Gillem grinned. "That's for sure."

"How you planning to get this thing to the harbor?" Mr. Caughlin asked.

Daddy laughed and shook his head. "I haven't quite figured that part out yet."

I saw looks pass all around, and before they left, the four men had made a date with Daddy. They'd carry the boat over the seawall first thing in the morning.

Daddy's eyes twinkled in the lamplight. While he shook their hands and offered his thanks, I realized how much those men admired his hard work and determination.

I thought again about Mama saying I had a lot of Daddy in me. Maybe it wasn't such a bad thing after all. Maybe what these men saw in Daddy was inside me, too.

I hoped it was so.

Chapter Eleven

WHEN I GOT UP for work the next morning, everyone got up. They all wanted to see Daddy's boat in the water. We must've been a sight, traipsing over that seawall. Mama led the way, a lamp in one hand and Bobby in the other. The men followed, two on each side of the boat, and Daddy made his way along the trail behind them. The rest of us kids brought up the rear.

From the top of the seawall, I saw a yellow moon hanging low in the eastern sky. It lit the cedars on the island across the harbor and glittered like rhinestones on the bay beyond. I soaked up the beauty of it, like I did every morning on my way to the cannery. Then I headed down the opposite trail.

The men sat the boat down at the edge of the dock. Mr. Gillem said he wished we had a bottle of champagne to do a proper launching, but Mr. Waller laughed at him.

"Now if we had champagne, Dan, the last thing we'd wanna do is waste it on John's boat. It ain't *that* purty."

They all laughed, then pushed the skiff into the glassy water. Mama's arm slid across Daddy's shoulder. I couldn't see their faces, but I knew they had to be happy. I was, too. Now there'd be fish to sell, and someday soon, with my help, there'd be enough money for the move back to Missouri.

When we could do no more, Mama and Daddy headed home with the kids, and the rest of us went to work. Once at the cannery, my fingers seemed to fly. Maybe it was seeing Daddy's boat in the water that spurred me on. Or last night's fiddle playing. Or maybe it was seeing all those men wanting to help Daddy. Whatever it was, I was grateful for it. I finished two full buckets and collected two nickels. Dollie clapped, and Mr. Gillem let out a whoop. It made me feel good, like I could do anything I set my mind to. I even saw Mr. Sparrow that day. He nodded at me from a table at the rear of the cannery. We never did speak, but I was relieved to know he was working. I hoped we'd both be free of our boxes before long.

Going home, I looked for Daddy's boat. I didn't see it sitting high in the water where we'd left it. I didn't see it anywhere. I ran to the dock, looked over the edge, and there it was, still tied to the piling but full of water, the edges barely above the surface.

"Mr. Gillem," I hollered. "Daddy's boat sank!" I dropped to my knees and tugged hard on the bowline. The boat wouldn't budge.

Mr. Gillem patted my arm. "It's all right, Sadie. It's supposed to do that."

I stared at him. "But boats aren't supposed to sink."

"You have to soak a new boat so the wood swells." He smiled down at me. "Stops the leaks."

I blinked at him, feeling foolish. A carpenter's daughter should know these things.

I stood up, trying to hide my embarrassment. "So how do you get it up?"

Mr. Gillem laughed. "You bail," he said. "Fast."

Daddy came down the seawall just then. Jacob and Oren ran ahead, carrying the bailing scoops Daddy had made from old apple boxes. From the looks on their faces, this was one job they didn't mind doing. Laughing, they jumped in beside the boat and started scooping, flinging water over the sides and at each other. The boat began to rise, and before long it was sitting high with only a half inch of water sloshing around the bottom. Daddy held out a hand and pulled first Oren, then Jacob, onto the dock. Water pooled around their feet.

"When you taking it out, Daddy?" Jacob asked. His wet hair spiked above his forehead like horns.

Daddy eyed the boat. "In the morning. If it doesn't fill again overnight."

Jacob blinked hard, his eyes red from the salty drenching Oren gave him. "Can I go with you?" he asked.

Daddy smiled and nodded. "You can."

Suddenly I wanted to go, too, but I didn't ask. I had my own job now. I couldn't take time out to go fishing with Daddy, even if he'd let me.

Jacob checked the boat at least a dozen times before dark, measuring the bit of water in the bottom to see how much it'd leaked since being bailed. And all evening he sat with Daddy, asking questions about the bay and about fishing. By bedtime, Daddy knew his boat was seaworthy. And before daylight, he and Jacob struck out for the harbor, carrying oars, cane poles, and Mama's sail.

Daddy's boat held up fine. Every morning a shrimp boat towed them out to South Bay or Hog

Island or sometimes East Flats, where Daddy and Jacob would fish all day before sailing home. Some days the catch was better than others, but Daddy always brought home money. Mama looked happy, and I guess I was, too. By the beginning of September, I'd saved a whole dollar and fifty-four cents.

It was a Sunday night before Labor Day that everything changed. Mr. Hauke gave us some worrisome news. A hurricane was brewing in the Gulf.

I remembered seeing a newsreel about a hurricane when we went to see *Tarzan, the Ape Man* at the picture show last year. They showed palm trees battered by wind and rain and whole houses being swept away. I looked around me. I didn't see how that could happen here, with the sun shining so hot and the sky so blue.

Labor Day morning turned steamy with the first rays of sunshine, and it didn't take long before my face felt red as boiled crabs. Sweat dripped from my nose and crawled down my back till my clothes stuck to me and I wished I were back at the cannery peeling icy cold shrimp. Nothing moved—not a bird or a cat, not even a dragonfly. Daddy said it was 'cause of the storm. He said animals and insects usually had more sense than people when it came to these things.

After breakfast, Mr. Gillem came walking across the lane with Davis and Mr. Waller. He smiled at

Mama, said "Morning, Raine," then turned a serious face to Daddy. "I think we'd better drag that new boat of yours into the cedars, John."

Daddy looked relieved. He called Jacob. "Think you can help these men?"

Jacob's chest swelled. "Yessir," he said.

"You'd better go with them, too, Sadie."

I nodded and headed toward the seawall behind the boys.

I figured today had to be the hottest I'd ever seen. With every step up the trail, my sweaty dress twisted and clung to me like a wet rag. And just when I thought the deathly still morning would never breathe again, I felt a sigh, a feeble little breeze whispering around my legs and fingering through my damp hair.

When we reached the top, I looked past the harbor to the bay. A deep-blue line floated on the horizon, as simple and innocent-looking as a piece of Mama's rug yarn. It looked far away, but I knew it was the storm coming. I glanced down the road, searching for Mr. Sparrow like I always did, but this time, I was comforted to find him gone. He needed to be someplace safe and dry tonight.

I followed Davis and Jacob down to the harbor road and felt the wind pick up. In a sudden rush, it billowed my skirt, swept back my sticky hair, and rustled through the cedars behind me. The air smelled different—sweet, like it came from far away. I stood there in the road with my eyes closed, breathing it in, feeling like I'd been whisked to a part of the world I'd never see except in dreams.

Davis tugged at my arm and brought me back. "Come on," he said, frowning. "We need to get this done."

I hurried across the road to the dock. The tide had risen, and when the wind gusted, it swept water over the bulkhead and splashed it at our feet. Daddy's boat pitched and thudded against the pilings. I cringed at the crunching, scraping sound and glanced down the harbor. Fish houses were boarded up, and men scurried over the decks of remaining boats, in a hurry to move them out of the harbor to safer inlets.

Mr. Gillem climbed into Daddy's boat, passed the sail and oars to Davis, and untied the bowline. It took all five of us to haul the soaked skiff out of the water and into the cedars. When the boat had been wedged tight in the trees, the men headed for home. I let them go and stood with Jacob and Davis to get a last look at the sky. The deep-blue line we'd seen earlier had stretched halfway across the bay, reaching for us like a great dark hand.

Chapter Twelve

"TIDE'S RISING," Mr. Gillem said, "and there's no telling where that storm's gonna come in. Better get your things and camp out at the schoolhouse with us."

Daddy frowned. "Is there someplace else we could go?"

I knew Daddy hated depending on anyone but himself. He was stubborn that way.

Mr. Gillem shook his head. "You might drive farther inland and do okay, but it would take a lot of gasoline."

Daddy glanced at the sky.

"Hope you're not thinking of staying, John. I've only been here a year, but I've already seen a foot of tidewater right where you're sitting, and that was just a small storm."

"When you going?" Daddy asked.

"Soon as Irene packs up what we can carry. Want to follow us into town?"

Daddy nodded, and Mr. Gillem waved, already headed across the lane.

Mama must've suspected we'd have to leave. When I stepped inside the house, I smelled biscuits baking, and she already had our bedding folded and stacked on the table. "You and Jacob get your things together," she said, grabbing a cup towel. "Then help me with the rest. We've got lots to do." She pulled steaming biscuits from the oven, put more in to bake, and went back to her packing.

Daddy and Jacob took down our lean-to and nailed the window boards shut on the house. Me and Mama worked fast as we could and loaded half of everything we owned into the car to take with us. Daddy complained that it was a foolish thing to do. "The car could blow away just like the house," he said.

I smelled rain coming, a sweet, earthy scent riding heavy on the wind, and the excitement of it quickened inside me. I couldn't remember the last time I'd seen rain. As I hurried to finish, big drops hit me on the head and arms and kicked up dust on the ground around me. Then in a rush the storm hit. We jumped in the car and sat there for a moment, watching the thundering raindrops hit the windows so hard I thought the glass would crack. It was like the sky had a hole in it and all of heaven's rain was pouring down on us.

Mr. Gillem pulled into the lane and waved at us, his truck cab crammed so full of kids, I didn't see how he could drive. Through the waterfall down my window, I watched them inch toward the road, wondering if Davis and Oren were under all those kids or huddled in the back beneath the hot wagon sheet, trying to keep dry.

We followed their truck into town, past the drugstore and the Jackson Hotel, and parked in front of the schoolhouse behind Mr. Gillem. I stared out the bleary window at Central Ward, the school I'd be attending next week. Rising two stories into the black sky, the brick building looked mean and unforgiving. Kinda like Miss Ira, my sixth-grade teacher back home, the only person in the world who could tie my stomach in a knot with a single look. Or Nadine Lowry, with her fancy shoes and shiny ribbons. If I didn't get inside right after the bell, she'd leave a handful of dirt on my seat every morning. I never did understand why she hated me so, unless it was 'cause Nate Bonner liked me better. My belly tightened up just thinking of her. Next Monday, I could be facing a whole school full of Nadines.

Kids poured out of the Gillem truck, arms loaded, and ran up the wide school steps and through the front door. I saw Davis and Oren jump from the truck bed, and Mr. Gillem, hunching over baby Caleb, ran after them.

"I guess we'd better go in," Mama said.

I could hardly hear her over the pounding rain. She wiped the fog from her window and peered at the sky. "It probably won't get any better than this."

Daddy nodded, but he didn't look happy. He'd get a soaking making his way along the ground to the schoolhouse door, but I knew that wasn't what bothered him most. He considered our staying at school charity, and he hated being on the receiving end of any kind of charity.

"Grab as much as you can carry," Mama said. "We sure don't want to forget something and have to come back out in this."

We divided up bundles and quilts, then bolted from the car. When I reached the safety of the front doors, I looked back through the pouring rain. Daddy's pants were already soaked, but the rest of him was dry thanks to Mama. Keeping pace with his swinging stride, she held a quilt above their heads till they reached the covered porch.

Once inside, the heavy doors banged shut behind us, muffling the noisy wind and rain. I shook off the water and looked around. The wide entry hall smelled of fresh paint and wax, and the polished cement floor reflected electric lights hanging from the high ceiling. Ahead, voices echoed off thick plastered walls.

We followed Mr. Gillem to the main hall, where families had gathered. Some sat on quilts with bags of clothing and provisions beside them. Others sat on the bare floor with nothing to get them through the uncertain time ahead. Mr. and Mrs. Gillem nodded and waved at almost everyone. I saw only a few familiar faces, but Mr. Sparrow's wasn't one of them.

Still dripping, we made our way down the hall to an empty space. Kids and grown-ups alike watched Daddy with their mouths gaped wide as hooked bass. I couldn't help but glare back at them. It was true Daddy's soaked pants left a trail on the floor like a giant snail, but Mama and Daddy would've scolded us to tears if we'd behaved like those folks. I wished the good Lord would see fit to teach them some manners. I glanced upward, wondering if God was listening. "A few flies down their gullets might work," I whispered.

Mama spread a quilt on the floor, and across from us, Mrs. Gillem did the same.

Dollie crossed to our side of the hall with another quilt and an old cigar box tucked under her arm. "We can sit together if you want. Get away from all these boys."

I looked at Mama, and she nodded.

So me and Dollie found a place by the last class-room, near the stairs at the end of the north hall. I helped spread our quilt, then peeked through the glass in the door. The clock on the wall read 10:08, but right in front of my eyes, the second hand stopped and the lights went out. The electricity was off.

I peered through the gloom at the tall windows streaked with rain, at the rows of desks, at the black-board, washed clean and ready for the first day of school. Butterflies started up in my stomach. They flapped and bumped around inside me till I felt plumb queasy. Come Monday, I'd be sitting in a room just like this one. A room full of Nadines, more than likely. And a teacher who would give me a Miss Ira look. I slumped beside Dollie and pulled in a deep breath.

"You feeling poorly?" she asked, setting her cigar box between us.

I shook my head. "It's nothing."

She frowned, stared at me a moment, then opened the box. "We're gonna be stuck here a long time, so I brought us something to do." She pulled out a checkered piece of paper colored in black and red crayon squares and poured bottle caps onto the quilt. "Which do you want?" she asked. "Nehi or Royal Crown?"

I looked at the caps and Dollie's wrinkled home-made checkerboard and tried to smile. "Nehi," I said.

While we played countless games of checkers throughout the long, dark day, I thought about how strange it was that I was sitting across from Dollie instead of Wilma. I still hadn't heard from her, and it worried me. She had promised to write as soon as she got my letter. I wondered if I might've gotten the address wrong. Wilma could be waiting, thinking I'd made new friends and didn't care about her any-more. It was an awful thought. She would need my help to get her through all the strangeness she was facing in California, and I knew I needed her.

So, when Dollie left to help her mama with the little ones, I unpacked my pencil and paper and wrote another letter. I addressed the envelope in neat block letters, double-checking to make sure it was right. This letter had to reach her, and this time, I could buy a three-cent stamp with my own money and mail it as soon as the storm was over.

With the sun hidden so far behind the clouds, it was impossible to tell what time of day it was. I figured it must be late. Shadows had thickened in corners, hunkered like sleeping cats, and mamas had begun to feed hungry kids their evening meal.

Jacob brought me my supper—biscuits with peanut butter. He dropped them on the quilt and hurried back to sit with the Gillem boys. I didn't have much appetite, but I ate them anyway. Mama would be mad if I didn't.

When Dollie came back, she plopped beside me and leaned against the door.

"Did I tell you this was Mrs. Cleming's room last year?" she asked. "She taught Oren fourth grade right here. Fifth through eighth are upstairs." She pointed toward the ceiling. "Wanna see?"

I glanced up and down the halls. "We'll get in trouble, won't we?"

"Naw," she said. "Come on."

I frowned, and Dollie giggled. She stood, stretched, and slipped around the corner. Startled, I looked at Mama. She was sewing, and Daddy was busy talking to Mr. and Mrs. Gillem. I scooted closer to the stairs and felt my stomach tighten up again. After another quick glance at Mama, I scrambled around the corner, my back to the wall, and looked up at Dollie leaning over the second-floor railing.

"Come on," she whispered, "before it gets too dark."

I tiptoed up the staircase, and at the top, I stared down another wide hallway lined with doors.

"This way," Dollie said.

She led me halfway down the long hall and eased open a door on the right.

"This was seventh grade last year," she said.

I leaned through the doorway, and as I peered inside, Dollie put a hand on my back and gave me a light push.

"Go on in and look around," she said.

I gasped and stumbled through, tossing frantic glances over my shoulders and all around. When I was satisfied we were alone, I shot Dollie a hard look. "Don't you ever do that again."

She flinched. "Didn't mean to startle you. Just wanted to ease your mind some, is all." She gave me an embarrassed look. "I remember how I felt when I first moved here. Starting school was scary."

"I'm not scared," I lied.

Dollie nodded. "I just thought you might be a little like me and—"

"Well, I'm not."

Dollie gave me such a bewildered look, I felt terrible. I didn't really mean to hurt her feelings. I was tired, that's all. Achy-tired of strange people and the idea of starting over in a new school. And tired of everyone on that bayfront thinking I was just like them 'cause I lived in a tar-paper shack. I didn't want to be like them. I wanted my old house. I wanted Wilma.

The wind picked up, hurling leaves and driving rain against the windows. Dollie walked past rows of desks and looked down at the street below. I thought she was mad at me, but she acted like nothing had happened at all. "I can see your car from up here," she said.

I followed her to the rain-streaked glass and peered through the gloom at our drowning car. It looked small beneath the towering schoolhouse—a scrap of black metal barely visible under the gray downpour. Kinda like me, I thought. Since moving to this place, I wasn't but a scrap of what I used to be, either. I'd been drowning, too, under a flood of tents and tar-paper shacks and big brick schoolhouses, and soon, a room full of Nadine Lowrys. I could see Nadine's smirking face in my head clear as day. Only this time I wouldn't have Wilma with me. I'd be alone.

Wind gusted, and rain slammed against the glass so hard I couldn't breathe. I needed out. I pushed away from the window, ran past the desks, and slammed smack into Davis. We hit the floor with a thud.

"Whoa," he said, pushing himself up. "What's the hurry?"

< 111 >

"Sorry. I didn't see you," I mumbled.

"Well, I'm glad of that. I'd hate to think you knocked me down on purpose."

"Were you looking for us?" Dollie asked him.

"Yeah. Mr. and Mrs. Wynn got worried when they couldn't see Sadie anywhere, so I told them I'd find her."

I leaned against the classroom wall. With all there was to worry about, Mama and Daddy's concern for my whereabouts struck me as funny. How far could I get with a hurricane blowing outside? I laughed. And when I saw puzzled looks pass between Dollie and Davis, I laughed again. It didn't matter what they thought of me anymore. Nothing mattered. I didn't care how many Nadine Lowrys there were in the world, or why Wilma hadn't written, or where Mr. Sparrow was sleeping tonight. I didn't even care where we lived. I was bone-tired of caring.

I hoped the storm would blow us all away.

Chapter Thirteen

WIND HOWLED and rain pounded all through that long, dark night. Babies cried and kids whimpered. Even grown men moaned in their sleep.

Seeing all this misery around me, I felt terrible. I should've never wished the storm would blow us away. And I *did* care if I made Mama and Daddy worry and if Wilma and Mr. Sparrow were safe. I hoped God knew that. I never meant for anyone to suffer. Mama was fond of reminding us that you reap what you sow. I snuggled closer to Bobby and hoped the awful words I'd sown earlier wouldn't bring doom on us all.

Finally, with the hallways damp and dim, morning came, and the storm eased a bit. I heard people stirring, whispering, fumbling for leftover biscuits or corn bread or beans.

Bobby whined, hungry, too, so Mama pulled out the last of our biscuits. She spread grape jelly through the middles and passed them around.

I still hadn't gotten my appetite back. I set my biscuits on the quilt and listened to the hushed voices around me. No one had much to say, unless it was about the hurricane. Or the Depression.

"Thirteen million men out of work," I heard a man say.

I tried to cipher that number, picturing people in groups of hundreds crowded into streets, spilling into farmland and meadows, all hungry and in need of work. But my head couldn't take in a number that big. It sounded like all the people in the world to me.

"Roosevelt's New Deal is supposed to drum up jobs for them," another said. "Too late to save my farm, though."

"But we're feeding our kids now," the first one said. "I seen grown men—musta been fifty of 'em— behind a restaurant in Chicago last spring, fighting over a barrel of garbage. And kids sleeping in the cold under Hoover blankets and scouring the dumps for food." He shook his head. "Don't matter what we lost, Will. Matters what we got now."

A young boy tugged at the man's sleeve. "What's a Hoover blanket, Papa?"

I wondered, too. Herbert Hoover had been our last president, but I'd never heard of a blanket named for him. I leaned closer to catch the man's answer.

"A newspaper, son. Just a newspaper."

I ran my hand over Mama's thick quilt. Then I picked up my biscuits and ate every bite. I wondered if Mr. Sparrow had lived in Chicago. If he'd lost his job, his house—everything—and had to leave his family to find work. I recalled the shiny-clean faces in his photograph and wondered where they were now, if the kids had enough to eat, if they were still alive, even. I glanced at Daddy. Maybe he feared we would've ended the same way if we hadn't left home.

Scraps of daylight crept through the classroom doors and washed pale squares of light along the hallway. People gathered their things and waited for the rain to stop.

Daddy itched to go. I heard him talking to Mr. Gillem about last night's strong winds, worried our house might've blown away. I couldn't bring myself to look at either of them, knowing I'd wished it on us all.

A hush swept down the halls, and I looked up to see a strange man standing not far from us. Rows of faces stared up at him, waiting.

< 115 >

"That there is Spits Cameron," Oren whispered to Jacob. "He's a deacon over at the Methodist church."

The man pulled his dripping hat from his head, and in a sorrowful voice, he told us about the storm.

"At one o'clock last night," he said, "the hurricane hit this side of Brownsville with eighty-mile-an-hour winds. We got high tides up the entire Texas coast." He shook his head and pulled in a ragged breath. "But that ain't the worst of it. Radio says a thirteen-foot wave killed as many as forty people near Brownsville and injured maybe fifteen hundred."

I heard gasps all around and saw Daddy slide his arm around Mama. I looked at the high ceilings, trying to picture a wall of water even higher crashing into the seawall and over our house. It was too horrible to imagine, and yet I couldn't stop thinking about it. I kept seeing Mama and Daddy, Jacob and Emily, and little Bobby tossed and churned through dark water, limp and lifeless as rag dolls.

I squeezed my eyes shut and prayed right then and there for forgiveness. I should've never wished that hurricane would blow us away.

"What about the seawall?" Mr. Gillem asked.

I held my breath and waited.

"I heard there were some breaks," the man said, "but I don't know where yet."

"What about the harbor?" someone asked.

"And the cannery?" shouted another voice.

The man shook his head. "That's all I know."

Gazes dropped to the floor, and no one said a word. The man turned his wet hat in his hands a few times, then strode through the front doors.

"Let's go," Daddy whispered.

Mama nodded and handed me quilts to fold. The Gillems were still eating breakfast, so Daddy told them we'd meet up with them later. We gathered our things and headed for the car.

Outside, last night's wind had scattered leaves and broken branches everywhere. Dark clouds still tumbled across the sky, but the storm was over. The rain had stopped as suddenly as it began. I scrambled into the car beside Emily, praying like everything that no one in Aransas Pass had died, and that Daddy's boat and our little black house were okay. After all my mean thoughts about this town last night, I was sure it'd be my fault if anything bad had happened.

We headed toward town and saw storekeepers prying boards from windows and sweeping dirty rainwater and rubbish from sidewalks. We turned east, and I held my breath rounding the corner, expecting to see the seawall washed away and all the houses with it. At the last second, I squeezed my eyes shut, too afraid to look till I heard Mama's relieved sigh.

< 117 >

The seawall was still there, so maybe our house was, too. But the closer we got to the railroad track, the worse the road looked. Water overflowed the ditches. Scraps of lumber and broken branches and old buckets floated everywhere. Daddy slowed the car to a crawl. I saw a dead hen, feathers ruffled with mud, and hoped the poor thing wasn't one of Mr. Caughlin's.

When we reached the tracks, Daddy had to stop. The road ahead looked like a river. Squinting past the gray water, I saw a shape hunkered in the shadowy corner of the seawall—our house—still standing, but too far away for me to see the damage.

Ahead of us, a few men waded through knee-deep water to check on their own houses. Jacob leaned over the front seat. "I could wade that water, too, Daddy," he said. "I could see about your boat and the house and be back quick as anything."

Daddy didn't answer.

"There might be snakes, John," Mama said.

Daddy watched the slow struggle of the wading men till they got to our lane. "It doesn't look that bad, Raine. He should go. We need to know."

"Don't worry, Mama," Jacob said. He kissed her on the cheek. "I'll take a stick with me and watch for snakes real careful-like."

He scrambled from the car, grabbed a stray limb floating at the side of the road, and took off. I watched him till he disappeared into the shadows of the seawall. After a while, he appeared again, trudging back through the water to the car. Mama and Daddy hadn't said a word since he left. Even Emily and Bobby were quiet. When Jacob got close enough, he hollered, "Everything's okay," and Emily and Bobby bounced on the seat, singing Jacob's words over and over till Mama had to hush them.

Up to that moment, I hadn't known just how much I wanted that tar-paper shack to still be there. Daddy's boat was safe, too, so we still had a way to make a living, a means of working our way back to Missouri.

I could finally breathe. Maybe God hadn't been too awfully mad at me after all.

Jacob climbed into the car, dripping smelly, muddy water all over the floorboard and seats. "The house looks okay, Daddy," he said. "We got tar paper missing, the roof leaked, and the dirt floor's turned muddy, but it's okay." He paused to catch his breath. "And your boat's just wedged in the cedars like we left it."

Daddy sighed deep and nodded.

"What do we do now?" Jacob asked.

"We wait for the water to go down," Daddy said.

He turned the car around and headed back to town. I was afraid he was taking us back to the schoolhouse, but he passed it up and kept going. We drove till the road turned to oyster shell, then dirt ruts, and finally ended.

Daddy pulled up close to some brushy live oak trees and built a fire in a clearing so Mama could cook a real meal. Later, he put up the tent. Like me, I guess he couldn't bear another night in that schoolhouse. I was thankful.

Throughout that long day, I tried hard to forget there'd ever been a hurricane. But when the sun came out, reminding me of picnics we had back home, my thoughts still ended up in front of that thirteen-foot wall of water. No matter how tightly I squeezed my eyes shut, I kept seeing mamas and daddies, kids and animals being swept away in that towering wave.

My heart ached for those lost souls. For the terror they must've felt. And for all the lonesome loved ones they left behind.

Chapter Fourteen

Two nights were all Daddy could stand in that place, and early that second morning, Mama's nudges woke me. "Time to get up," she said. "Daddy wants breakfast done and over so we can pack up and go."

For a moment, I thought we were back on the road, traveling to Texas. The rising sun shone through the tent flap like all was right with the world, but it didn't take long before memories of the storm came flooding back. I washed up, heavy with the recollection of it all.

I helped Mama with breakfast while Daddy and Jacob packed up the tent, and before the sun had time enough to rise above the trees, we were finished eating and back in the car. Daddy said he'd stop at the post office so I could mail my letter to Wilma. I was relieved and made note of the date. This time I was sure of the address, and sure, too, I'd probably hear from her in a few weeks.

The two days of sunshine had made a difference in town. Cement sidewalks were dry, and store windows shone. It gave me hope that maybe we could get back to normal, too. I mailed my letter, and we headed home.

When we reached the tracks, I knew it'd be a while before things would be normal for us again. The standing water had gone down some, but the road still looked like a river. Up ahead, Mr. Gillem's empty truck sat parked off the main road, close to our lane. I knew when Daddy saw it he'd try to do the same, even though he'd be waist-deep in muddy water when he got out. Sure enough, he eased forward and crept down the road.

Water splashed over the running board, and branches and rubbish drifted past us. When Daddy spotted three wide boards caught in the brush at the side of the road, he stopped the car and called to Jacob.

"Think you could float those boards back to the house?"

Jacob reached for the door handle. "Yessir," he said, and scooted into the murky water.

While Emily and Bobby watched Jacob out the rear window, we inched ahead and finally reached the Gillem truck. Daddy paused, thoughtful-like, then pointed the car toward our lane. Mama sucked in a breath, and I did, too. The deeper water at the side of the road lapped at the doors and leaked through, trickling onto the floorboard. But after the big dip, we pulled up onto the lane and drove straight to the house.

Daddy parked out of the water on the rise beside the chinaberry tree. The tree was a sad thing to see, with its limbs bony and bare. Our house wasn't any better. The new tar paper hung in tattered strips, and inside, damp cardboard sagged, dark and smelly. All our work had gone to waste. I kicked the doorjamb. Mama frowned, but I didn't care. Seemed to me that all of nature had schemed against us from the beginning. First with a drought, then a flood. Like it had a problem with our wanting to just breathe.

The Gillems hadn't fared any better. They'd already pulled off their ragged tar paper and piled wet cardboard in the yard to burn later. As far as I could see, all the houses down our lane had suffered the same fate.

"Found another one, Daddy," I heard Jacob holler.

I turned and saw him pushing four long boards out of the water onto the rise.

Daddy nodded and took another look inside the house. "Jacob," he called. "Get my rule out of the car."

When Jacob came back, Daddy had us measure the width and length of the house. He picked up a stick, did some figuring in the dirt, then started back to the car.

"Well, come on," he said. "We got lumber to buy."

I glanced at Mama. She looked as surprised as I felt.

"You heard your daddy," she said. "Get in the car."

Jacob leaned close. "I reckon we're gonna get a new floor," he whispered in my ear.

I grinned, but I had to wonder how Daddy could do it. Lumber was expensive.

We eased back onto the lane and crept through the deep water at the edge of the road. I wasn't sure our old car would make it without stalling, but it did, and moments later we were headed back to town.

We waited while Daddy went inside the lumber-yard. In a short while he was hauling himself onto the seat again. "Couldn't get it all, Raine," he said. "But I got cardboard, tar paper, and enough lumber for half the floor. The rest will have to wait."

"They don't mind driving through water to deliver?"

Daddy shook his head and turned toward our flooded road. "Mr. Fields said he'd send it out today."

Emily giggled, and Jacob jabbed an elbow in my ribs. I was excited, too. Half a floor was better than none at all. At least we could sleep high and dry.

Then I thought about the money in my mason jar, the growing weight of it, the clinking sound the coins made when I added each day's pay. I had a dollar and fifty-four cents saved. I could give it all to Daddy.

I'd often imagined the way Daddy would look when I handed him my mason jar filled to the brim. He'd look surprised at first. Then I'd see the corners of his mouth curve in a wide grin. And then his eyes would shine, brighter than the first time I made all A's in school.

No, I decided. We could make do with half a floor. It would be better to save my money for the trip back home.

Daddy pulled down our lane and onto the rise. He said we'd be staying in the tent while he worked on the floor, but before we set up camp, we'd need to push the boat back into the water.

When we reached the top of the seawall, I saw that Mr. Sparrow's box was gone. I never expected it to survive the storm, but I'd wondered if Mr. Sparrow would replace it. Before I could give him another thought, Jacob asked, "Where's the boat?" I checked the cedars where we'd left it, and my heart nearly froze in my chest. Daddy must've felt the same way 'cause his eyes flashed, then narrowed to slits. His boat was gone.

It was an awful moment. But when we peered down at the harbor, we saw the boat tied to the dock, floating smooth and steady like there'd never been a storm.

"Looks like we had some help while we were gone," Daddy said, smiling.

Emily peered down at the boat, lifted her chin, and in her best imitation of Daddy, she said, "Must've been fairies."

Daddy busted out laughing.

When we got back to the house, we went to work. Mama put on a pot of beans while Daddy and Jacob set up camp. I got busy tearing down the ruined cardboard. By the time we'd ripped away the last of the ragged tar paper, we saw a lumber truck plunging through the floodwater. It pulled onto our lane, creaking and groaning, and stopped in front of the house.

"Mr. Wynn?" the driver asked.

Daddy nodded.

The man glanced at his piece of paper. "I got your

nails, tar paper, seventeen joists, three hundred and sixty-four board feet of pine, and Mr. Fields said you're to get this here stack of scrap cardboard."

"You got too much lumber," Daddy said. "I ordered half that much."

The man shrugged. "All I know is Mr. Fields said to deliver it and he'd settle up with you later. He said you could return anything you don't need."

Mama stifled a smile with her hand.

The man waited.

I was sure daddy would send it back. I heard him say once that credit wasn't much different than pity or charity. But to my surprise he nodded and pointed to the dry space between the house and the tent. "You can put it there," he said.

"Yes, sir."

The man unloaded his truck, and when he was gone, I asked Mama why Daddy took the credit Mr. Fields offered.

"Your daddy's proud, but he'd never put pride above his family."

I nodded. "But why did Mr. Fields do that for Daddy?" I asked.

Mama smiled. "Who you are inside always shows, Sadie. Mr. Fields knows he'll be paid."

I nodded again like I understood, but Mama's answer only stirred more questions in me. I guess

Mr. Fields saw something in Daddy he could trust right off. Maybe that's what she meant. But it didn't sit well with me that who I was inside might be shining like a marquee at a picture show for anyone to see.

It wasn't fair that a stranger could see what I didn't even know myself.

Chapter Fifteen

THE FOUR O'CLOCK WHISTLE didn't blow Friday morning. The newspaper reported that the cannery had suffered three thousand dollars in storm damage, most of it to the peeling room. I said the amount out loud, trying to get a feel for how much three thousand dollars might be, but I couldn't even imagine a pile of money that big.

The cannery went to work repairing their building, but it would still be Monday before the peeling room was back in business. As much as I wanted to keep adding to my mason jar, I knew I couldn't be there when the doors opened. Monday was the first day of school, and just thinking about that big brick building made my belly quiver.

We started work on the house right away. The Gillems needed their ladder for their own repairs, so Daddy built us one. He tested it himself, sitting on each rung just long enough to pull himself up to the next. He was up that ladder quicker than you could shoo a fly. He checked the roof, and, satisfied that the rafters were sound, he left us to do the papering and started work on the floor.

Up on the roof, I could see the road all the way to the tracks—a piece of it, anyway. A narrow strip of muddy oyster shell nosed between the overfull ditches. I saw Davis and Oren across the way, too, papering their house. Davis looked up from his work, his face shining with sweat, and waved. I waved back.

Daddy worked hard—harder than he had on the boat. Mama said he wanted the floor finished quick so he could get back to fishing. He wouldn't rest easy till Mr. Fields was paid in full.

He set joists that day, and early Saturday morning, he began sawing boards for the floor. Before supper, the work was done, and the house smelled of pine lumber. He sat in the middle of his new floor and grinned his "watermelon grin," as Mama liked to call it. Wide and sweet. I was happy, too, but wondered why we had so many boards left over. When I asked Daddy about it, I got a wink. "You'll see," he said.

Me and Jacob got most everything moved in, and

< 130 >

after supper I helped Mama hang Daddy's fiddle and the rest of her pretty things on the fresh cardboard walls.

That night, Daddy told Jacob he could pick the next book for our reading. We all knew what that would be, even Daddy. With a grin, he watched Jacob go to the shelf and pull out *The Swiss Family Robinson*. Daddy must've read that book to us a dozen times, but we never tired of hearing about the shipwrecked family's adventure. I got to thinking while he read that in many ways we'd been ship-wrecked, too, right here by this seawall. We'd given up everything familiar to us and started a new life, just like the Robinsons.

When Daddy finished the first chapter, we went to bed with the sweet scent of new lumber around us. For the first time since we left home, I had something other than an old wagon sheet between me and the bare ground.

The pine boards felt clean and smooth, and I lay there in the dark with my hand off the edge of the quilt, just feeling them. But with only one more day left between me and Monday, it didn't take long for school to root out every nice thought in my head. One more day and I'd be walking into that school-house with all those strange kids—them knowing everyone and how everything worked.

And me knowing nothing.

Mama had us up and out of the house first thing the next morning. She said Daddy and Jacob needed room to work. Daddy started measuring and sawing right away while I helped Mama with breakfast. After we ate, he went right back to work. It wasn't till I was cleaning up breakfast dishes that I remembered Mr. Sparrow. With so much going on, I hadn't thought to check on him again. Now, the worry of not knowing his fate twisted around inside me till I thought I'd split wide open if I didn't take another look at that seawall.

When the dishes were done, I left Mama with her sewing and slipped away. All the way up the trail, my hope flitted like butterflies from one yearning to the next. I hoped to see another box. Then I hoped I wouldn't. Mr. Sparrow deserved more than a cardboard box to sleep in.

At the top, I looked all around, but I saw nothing. For a moment, fear welled up inside me, big as that awful wave that drowned all those poor Brownsville people. What if Mr. Sparrow had drowned, too? What if he'd been carried off with the tide? He had no family. No one to miss him.

Just me.

But when I thought about it, I knew this couldn't be. Mr. Sparrow struck me as smart, like Daddy.

He wouldn't be foolish enough to get caught in a storm.

Even so, I wondered if I should talk to Daddy about him.

I heard hammering again. I needed to get back. I scooted down the trail, but even before I reached the house, I'd decided not to say anything. Though me and Mr. Sparrow had never swapped a word, I knew Daddy wouldn't like hearing of my worry. Proper-raised girls didn't worry after strange men.

I got back in time to help Jacob take down the tent. We stretched it between the house and chinaberry tree like before, and when we finished, I sat in the shade beside Mama. She was working on the morning-glory flour sacks she brought with us from Missouri. I especially liked this print 'cause the flowers reminded me of the blue dress Wilma wore the day I last saw her. She always looked her best in blue.

"Are your chores finished?" Mama asked.

I nodded, and she handed me a needle and thread.

"Then you can hem the new underwear," she said.

I'd been doing hems on underwear since I was eight. I didn't care much for sewing, and my stitching showed it, but Mama insisted that I keep practicing. I guess she figured my uneven stitches wouldn't matter much in the underthings.

< 133 >

I worked a lot slower than Mama, and it took me the rest of the morning and part of the afternoon to finish up the little I had to do. I was almost done when a sandy-haired boy showed up, asking Daddy for a job. He introduced himself as Aubrey Denton. I'd seen him a few times before and knew he lived at the end of our lane.

"Mr. Waller mentioned you might be needing help," he said, squirming under Daddy's gaze. "Seeing as how your son won't be around 'cept on weekends on account of school and all."

This surprised me. I'd been so busy thinking about the storm and school, I hadn't thought once about Daddy having to manage without Jacob's help.

Daddy frowned. "How old are you? Twelve? Thirteen?"

"Just turned thirteen, sir."

"And why aren't you going to school tomorrow with the rest of the kids?"

"I got me a family that needs me more than that schoolhouse does." He dug his bare toes into the dirt. "If you could use me, sir, I'd work hard for you."

Daddy rubbed the stubble on his chin, staring at poor Aubrey till I thought the boy would squirm himself right into the ground. Finally Daddy nodded.

"Mind you, this wouldn't be a real job till I see how you do."

Aubrey's grin was bright as Mrs. Hauke's electric light. "Yessir," he said. "Will you be fishing tomorrow, sir?"

Daddy nodded. "Be here a bit after the whistle blows, and we'll give you a try. And wear a hat. Don't want you getting burned."

"Yessir. Thank you, sir. I'll be here." He shook Daddy's hand and ran off down the lane.

Smiling, Daddy watched him go, then turned to gather his tools. That's when I realized he must be finished with his surprise. Jacob stood in the doorway, grinning.

"All done?" Mama asked.

When Daddy nodded, Emily and Bobby ran toward the door, bumping and shoving to see what he had built. I left the new underwear on the bench and hurried after Mama.

At first I didn't know what to think. In the back third of the house I saw a platform built from wall to wall about five feet off the floor. And off to one side Daddy had fastened the ladder he'd built to the wall.

"The rafters are too low to build it high as I would've liked, but it's a sleeping loft, nonetheless," he said. "Big enough for all you kids to stretch out." He pointed underneath. "Me and Mama will sleep down here."

"Can we see?" Emily asked.

Bobby squirmed. "Can we, Daddy?"

Daddy nodded, and we scooted up the ladder. Even bent over, I brushed against the cardboard on the rafters, but sitting down, there was plenty of headroom. Bobby could stand up straight.

"Don't fall over that edge," Mama called to him. But Bobby danced around, too excited to listen.

We sprawled out in pecking order, trying out the space.

"Look, Daddy!" Bobby hollered. He moved his hands and feet like he was making snow angels. "We've got lots of room."

"I think you should put a rail up, John," Mama said.

Daddy laughed. "You couldn't *push* those kids out of bed, Raine."

But Mama said she wouldn't sleep a wink worrying, so Daddy went back to work.

There wasn't much left of the lumber, but he scrounged a single rail for Bobby's side of the loft. He even pieced together a quilting frame out of scraps for Mama. He rigged it to the rafters with tent cording so she could raise it to the ceiling when she wasn't quilting.

Mama was so happy with her surprise, she stopped making biscuits. She grabbed Daddy's face and planted a big kiss on his cheek, right there under the lean-to. We laughed. He looked funny with flour handprints sprouting from his ears.

After supper, Mama sat in her rocker and sewed blue rickrack around the collar and sleeves of my morning-glory dress. Right away, I knew this would be the one I'd wear tomorrow. The blue flowers made me feel like a piece of Wilma was with me. "It's really pretty, Mama," I said, looking at the hundreds of perfect stitches. "Pretty as any store-bought dress."

She patted me on the hand and went back to sewing.

When she was done, I heated up the iron on the camp stove and pressed my new dress. I hung it on a nail by the loft, then pulled out my old oxfords. After a thorough scrubbing, the shoes looked much better. I folded my socks, tucked them inside the shoes, and set them under my dress. When I turned around, I saw Jacob looking at his new shirts. He caught me watching and walked off like nothing could ruffle his feathers. But I knew he was fretting about school, same as me. It would be easier for him, though. He had Oren and all those boys, so he'd do fine. He didn't have a promise to keep.

Later that night, stretched out in our new loft, I thought about Dollie. She'd always been nice to me, done all the things a good friend would do, even offered to help me register tomorrow.

I felt a twinge of guilt, a nipping at my heels like walking in shoes too small for my feet. I wished things could be different between us. Dollie deserved better. But I just couldn't break my promise to Wilma.

Chapter Sixteen

I SMELLED PANCAKES and realized Monday morning was here. I'd be getting ready for school in a little while. I looked over the edge of the loft. Mama had made Daddy's breakfast and packed extra pancakes for him to take fishing.

Aubrey knocked on the door just seconds after the four o'clock whistle. Daddy shook his head and grinned. "The boy must've been waiting on the front step," he said.

I lay there till I heard them leave, then slipped down the loft ladder.

"Up so early?" Mama asked.

She gave me that look of hers—the one that sees clear through to the most secret parts. I nodded.

"Thinking about school?" she asked.

I nodded again, but I couldn't look her in the eye.

"I remember how it was for me," she said, reaching for a cup towel. "I changed schools more often than God changes seasons. And sometimes I didn't get to go at all."

Mama's daddy had been a horse trader during her growing years. They traveled from town to town, living out of a wagon, but till now I'd never stopped to think what that might've meant for her.

"Was it hard going to new schools all the time?"

Mama snapped the clean cup towel and spread it over her bowl of pancake batter. "Going," she said, her gaze fixed on those long-ago days, "wasn't nearly as bad as not going."

I stood there while this new thought shifted around inside me. I considered what it would be like to watch kids head off to school every morning without me, to never set foot in a classroom again. It didn't take long to see the foolishness in that. I liked school. I even made A's most of the time. It was the Nadine Lowrys and Miss Iras I didn't like.

When the kids woke up, Mama made a big stack of pancakes. She sprinkled the extra ones with sugar, rolled them up, and put them in paper sacks for school. Jacob dressed fast and sat on the floor, studying his shoes. He finally pushed them aside, grabbed

< 140 >

his sack, and scurried off barefoot to find Oren. I guess he figured that with the road still half-flooded, shoes would be too troublesome. Mama frowned, but he was out the door before she could complain.

I was dressed and waiting when Dollie knocked. Her short curls, damp but drying, stuck out in fuzzy ringlets all over her head.

She eyed my new dress. "You look real pretty this morning," she said.

I grinned and patted her springy red hair. "You do, too," I said, surprised I really meant it.

While she chatted with Mama, I realized that Dollie had a shine about her. Not a trifling little shine, mind you, but deep and bright. Bright as the light coming from Daddy's polished fiddle. I didn't know why I hadn't noticed it before. Even with all her freckles, even in her faded dress, she was pretty. I remembered what Mama said about who you are on the inside always showing, and I had to wonder what people saw in me. I smoothed my new dress and hoped Mama's fine needlework hadn't gone to waste.

When I opened the door, I saw Davis waiting at the edge of our muddy lane with his younger brothers, Wyatt and Ethan. Jacob had found Oren, and the two of them had already waded the overfull ditch and headed down the dry strip of road.

Davis's eyes lit up when he saw me. The look made my cheeks flush hot, only this time, blushing didn't make me mad at all. This time Davis made me feel that, just maybe, I had a little shine of my own.

Noise spilled through the open doorway at Central Ward even before we reached the steps. The clamor sounded more like a flock of hungry gulls than kids, but even so, my belly pitched and rolled with renewed dread. Davis pushed through eight grades of kids, clearing a path for us to the bulletin board.

"Mrs. Doogan is teaching seventh grade this year," he shouted to us over the noise. "Oren and Jacob have Miss Myers, and I've got"—he spread his arms wide like he was announcing a tightrope walker at the circus—"sweet Sweeney."

I smiled, but worry crawled all over me. Davis clearly didn't think Miss Sweeney was all that sweet. Maybe Mrs. Doogan wasn't, either.

"Better get Sadie and Jacob registered," he said. "Won't be long till the bell."

Dollie nodded and pushed toward the office. When the secretary was through with us, we left to find our rooms.

Dollie must've talked to a dozen kids on the way. Most of them I'd seen around our lane, but I thought it curious that everyone else seemed to look right through us. We ended up in the classroom Dollie had shown me during the storm. Jacob and Oren were across the hall, and Davis disappeared through the very last door by the south stairs.

I was thankful to see that Mrs. Doogan didn't look a thing like Miss Ira. Short auburn spit curls framed her plump cheeks, and once she even smiled at me. Miss Ira had never smiled. From the first day I saw her, her lips stayed puckered tight as the knot of gray hair on the back of her head.

I sat at a desk close to the door, and Dollie slid into the seat behind me. Leaning forward, she whispered that we wouldn't be together long. Alphabetical order ruled the classrooms. With names like Gillem and Wynn, we'd be seated on opposite sides of the room for sure. But Mrs. Doogan didn't move us that morning. It was like she understood how hard the first day of school could be, like she knew we needed friends close by even if we couldn't talk during class. I figured with a teacher like that, I could probably handle two Nadine Lowrys.

My butterflies eased a bit. The morning disappeared, and when the dinner bell rang, everyone went to the playground to eat. Dollie pulled me past the cement steps, past a girl from our room named

Claudia Yates who was sitting with a tight group of friends. We walked to a nearby live oak tree and sat in the shade. I opened my brown paper sack, but I couldn't keep my eyes off those girls. They chittered like squirrels, giggling and complimenting each other on new shoes and new dresses while they pulled out fat sandwiches made of light bread and bologna. I slid out my rolled-up pancake and saw them look my way. They put their heads together, then pulled back and laughed, Claudia louder than any of them. The sound sent shivers through me. I stuffed my pancake back in my paper sack.

Dollie frowned around her peanut-butter biscuit. "Aren't you hungry?" she mumbled, her mouth full.

I shook my head and nodded to the far corner of the playground. "Tomorrow," I whispered, "let's eat out there."

Before the last bell that evening, Mrs. Doogan had seated the whole seventh grade—all thirty-two of us—in alphabetical order. I ended up in the back by the windows with Claudia Yates behind me and Gunther Tyler in front. Claudia, in her store-bought dress and matching hair ribbon, took her desk without a single glance my way.

Just as well, I thought. Her shiny shoes reminded me of Nadine.

Gunther, tall and thin, had difficulty doing more

than keeping his long legs out of trouble. The moment his attention strayed, he'd relax, and his leg would stretch down the aisle ready to trip up the next pair of feet coming his way. I decided it was best to steer clear of him. And Claudia, too.

I barely had time to copy our first homework assignment from the blackboard before the last bell rang. I was glad to be leaving. I wanted to get home, where I didn't have to think about school for a while. Me and Dollie caught up with the rest of the kids outside the north entrance and started the long walk home. My stomach rumbled. I hadn't eaten since breakfast. Once we were clear of the schoolhouse, I pulled out my pancake and shared it with Wyatt, who always seemed to be hungry.

Before we reached our lane, Emily and Bobby ran to meet us. The Gillem kids waved good-bye and cut across the soggy empty lot to their house.

"Was school fun?" Bobby asked, his voice breathy from the run.

Jacob frowned. "Oh, sure. It was just keen," he muttered.

I stared at him, surprised at the sourness in his voice.

"I get to go next year," said Emily.

"Me too," Bobby said.

Emily put her hands on her hips. "No, you don't. You're too little."

"Nuh-*uh*." Bobby's short legs worked to catch up to Jacob. "I'm not too little, am I, Jacob?"

Jacob squatted in the middle of the lane and grabbed Bobby's shoulders. "You're not too little. Just too young. You're as good as anybody, you hear?"

Bobby nodded, and Jacob took off for the house. I stood there, staring after him.

"See," Bobby told Emily. "Jacob says I'm not too little."

When we got to the lean-to, Daddy was busy scaling a dozen small trout for supper.

"How was the fishing today, Daddy?" Jacob asked.

"Good. Aubrey's gonna work out fine."

"Wish I could've gone with you."

"You can go this weekend," Daddy said. "How was school?"

Jacob's face went white. He looked like every word in his head had been plucked right out and scattered to the winds.

"School was fine," I said, jumping in. "I got a real nice teacher."

Jacob let out a slow breath and found his voice. "Yessir," he said. "Me too." He grabbed the water buckets and ran out the door. "Better get these filled," he hollered over his shoulder. He took off toward the road like the devil was after him. Then he slowed to a shuffling gait.

I studied him till he disappeared behind Mrs. Kendall's house to fill the buckets. I was sure something had happened at school today. And sure, too, that Jacob had no intention of talking about it.

< 147 >

Chapter Seventeen

I MADE GOOD GRADES right from the start, but no matter how hard I studied, I couldn't beat Lucy Peardon. Dollie said I shouldn't waste my time worrying about it. "No one makes better grades than Lucy," she said. "Her mama's a high-school teacher."

Lucy seemed likeable enough, but it didn't take long before I noticed a rift deep as a canyon running between our side of the tracks and the town kids. To be fair, lots of them were nice, like Lucy, but plenty others never talked to us, never even looked at us unless they thought we weren't watching. Then I'd hear snickers and whispers. Dollie heard them, too, but she never seemed to let it trouble her. She'd just shrug and tell me, "Papa says some people can't feel tall unless they're stepping on someone else."

I wished I could see it that way, but being lumped into the same stewing pot with everyone on that bayfront made me mad. They were good people who didn't deserve to be treated so poorly, but we weren't like them at all. We had a nice home once, one I planned to see again someday.

By Wednesday I was anxious to get back to work. I wanted to add to my mason jar, but I also hoped to see Mr. Sparrow. Daddy said I could work before school as long as Mr. Gillem didn't mind and I got back in time to help Mama with morning chores.

So when the whistle blew Thursday morning, I headed to the cannery with Davis and Mr. Gillem. With so many little brothers, Dollie had to help out at home. I missed her, but all the way over the seawall and down the harbor road, all I could think about was seeing if Mr. Sparrow had made it through the storm okay.

Inside the cannery doors, I scanned faces at each table, looking for him. I watched the double doors, thinking he might be late. I kept an eye on the wide docking bays where boats unloaded their catch. But he wasn't anywhere.

Maybe he moved on, I told myself. Maybe he found a better job. I wanted to believe that, but my

< 149 >

heart clenched tight with worry. It must've shown all over me 'cause Davis gave me a puzzled look and glanced behind him, trying to see what it was I was fretting over. He finally took his place across the table from me, but every now and then, he'd peer around the cannery like he was trying to figure it out. I had to push Mr. Sparrow to the back of my mind to get my one bucket of shrimp headed and peeled.

I left Davis still working, collected my pay, and hurried home. Besides my promise to help with chores, I was nervous about getting the stink of shrimp off me. My clothes were wet and smelly, and I'd have to change and scrub up good before going to school. I was disappointed that I hadn't seen Mr. Sparrow. I'd look again tomorrow, but for now, the clink of another nickel in my mason jar would have to do.

But Mr. Sparrow didn't come to the cannery the next day. Or the next. I watched for him on my way to school. In the streets. In the post office. At the store. It was like he'd clean disappeared. I feared he might be hurt or sick from weathering the storm, curled up somewhere with no one to care for him. I just couldn't abide the idea of him being alone and friendless.

That last thought surprised me some. I guess I hadn't realized what had been at the heart of my worry till that moment. I always thought it was his eating and sleeping I fretted about. But from the first day I saw Mr. Sparrow, it had really been the loneliness in him that haunted me. The way it sat so heavy on his shoulders and slowed his feet to a shuffle. When I looked into his sad blue eyes that first day, I felt it, too, that ache of his from being alone in the world, the same kind of loneliness I'd felt being without Wilma.

That night in my prayers, I asked God to make sure Mr. Sparrow had a friend. A good friend, like I had in Wilma.

Over the next few weeks I tried to ignore Claudia, but it was hard. She wasn't choosy about who she picked on, and it didn't help that I sat right in front of her, unable to see what mischief she might be creating. One day we filed down the aisle after the last bell, and she slipped a drawing of Mrs. Doogan on my desk, complete with horns and a forked tail. Being the last one out, she could do most anything and not get seen. If I hadn't gone back for my history book, Mrs. Doogan would've found that awful picture and thought I'd done it for sure. After that, Dollie helped me keep watch.

But the tricks weren't the worst of it. Claudia's snide laughter cut deep and festered. Dollie said it was 'cause I was new that Claudia picked on me. It made me wonder if Jacob had been teased the same way. He hadn't said anything further about that first day at school, but he kept to himself more. Maybe he'd found a way to stop all those bad feelings from bothering him, the way Dollie did. I just wished I could, too.

As September disappeared, I kept watch for Wilma's letter, but each passing day brought no word from her. I didn't think it likely that two letters had been lost, but I couldn't bear the other possibility—the prospect that she might not want me as a friend anymore. The thought ate at me till I picked up my pencil and paper and started a third letter. I asked her to answer quick, just so I'd know she'd gotten my first letters okay. I mailed it to her the next day, and after a few weeks, I checked the post office every evening after school.

While I watched the days slip by, I flitted between worry for Wilma and being just plain mad that she might've broken her promise. But soon October was almost gone, and I had to face the fact that Wilma might be, too. I didn't really believe she'd break her promise, that new friends would've kept her from writing, but I knew something must've happened— something we hadn't planned on. Maybe her family had to move again, all of them, before I could send my new address. My letters might be sitting in that California post office right now, unclaimed.

I remembered the big wall map of the United States that Mrs. Doogan pinned up by the blackboard, the miles and miles of country stretched out in blocks of pink and green, blue and yellow. Black letters crawled across every state, marking thousands of towns and cities.

The hopelessness of my situation finally sank in. Wilma could be anywhere. But mostly she was gone.

I didn't know what to do. It didn't seem possible that Wilma could really be lost to me. But remembering how she looked that last day, the way she had pleaded with me to keep my promise, I knew in my heart there couldn't be another explanation. She would've answered my letters by now if she could've.

I was really alone. Wilma had disappeared, and it seemed that the very last part of me I could still recognize had disappeared with her. I was a stranger in this new place, even to myself.

I tried hard to put Wilma out of my mind, but before long, the pain of losing her got all mixed up with my worry for Mr. Sparrow and the bitterness Claudia had started. I felt it creeping inside me, oozing like mud along flooded creeks and riverbanks. I feared it might be changing me. Dirtying the bit of shine Davis saw in me that first day of school. Muddying me up till I'd never shine again.

I stumbled through the last week of October, filled with an emptiness so heavy I could hardly move through my days. And the nights, full of wondering what to do about my promise to Wilma, weren't any better. I had hoped that Daddy's Bible verses would have an answer for me, but I guess he didn't come across anything that applied to my particular problem. I finally figured I'd have to leave it in God's hands.

"Please watch over her," I asked in my prayers, "and help me find a way to keep my promise."

Chapter Eighteen

Ducks and geese dotted the bays and filled the skies with great, winged Vs. Daddy built duck blinds with Mr. Gillem, and soon there'd be meat to can and feathers to collect for mattresses.

The evening before Halloween, Mama said we'd be going to the dump at the edge of town to gather old mayonnaise and pickle jars. "If Daddy's hunts are as bountiful as he thinks," she said, "we'll be doing lots of canning."

Jacob's face soured the moment Mama told him where we were going. But he did as he was told and cut a few cedar branches for foraging. I didn't like the idea of rooting around the dump, either, but I spread rags on the back floorboard for dirty jars and helped Bobby and Emily put on their shoes.

Mama drove outside of town and parked at the edge of the dump. We sat there for a moment while flies buzzed and the smell of rotten vegetables breezed through the car windows. Mama shook her head. "With so many hungry, looks like stores and cafés would give it away before they let it ruin." She opened her door and seagulls flapped away, fussing 'cause we'd interrupted their scavenging. I watched them flutter overhead, calling back and forth, waiting for us to move on.

"Come on," Mama said.

She handed each of us a stick as we filed from the car.

"Let's get this done and get back home. I've still got supper to cook."

After stern reminders to stay away from the rotten vegetables and watch for broken glass, we began our search for pickle and mayonnaise jars. We poked around rusty tin cans and old bottles, busted lampshades and worn-out shoes, and after a while, we'd gathered more than a dozen jars. I didn't see much else that was any good and figured the dump must be picked over on a regular basis. Someone always needed scrap lumber for building or wood for cook fires.

But Jacob found an empty Coca-Cola bottle and an apple crate busted on one end. And I saw Mama ripping white buttons off an old shirt to use in her sewing. I found something, too. A small blue bottle. It wasn't good for much except being pretty to look at, but when Emily saw it, she stared at it like it was made of sapphires. I gave it to her and Bobby pouted. "I didn't find nothing good," he complained.

Jacob rolled his dirty jars onto the floorboard and held up his Coca-Cola bottle. "See this, Bobby?" he said. "If you stop your bellyaching, I'll sell this bottle and we'll all split some peppermint sticks."

Bobby finally grinned, and Mama said we'd done enough for one day.

When we got home, Mama started supper while I washed the dirty jars in boiling soapy water. With new sealing lids, they'd be good as store-bought. Emily washed her bottle, too, and insisted on setting it beside Grandma's rose-patterned teapot. It didn't seem fitting to me, putting a junk bottle next to something as special as that teapot, but Mama didn't mind. "Your grandma always did like blue," she said.

On the way home from school the next day, I had to remind myself that it was Halloween. Live oaks had leafed out again after the storm, and Mr. Gillem said they'd stay green right through winter. It seemed odd to me. Only a rare cottonwood or chinaberry tree had put on fall colors.

We walked along the shady sidewalk past the Jackson Hotel, and I remembered how it was back in Missouri this time of year. If I were home, harvest-colored leaves would be rustling and swirling around my feet. I missed seeing my breath puff clouds into chill mornings. And the sound of frost crunching underfoot. And the smell of wood smoke hanging in the air.

I wiped sweat from my upper lip. All we had here was sticky-damp wind and heat, and trees that never seemed to drop their leaves.

Wyatt showed off the orange pumpkin he'd colored in class, and Ethan made sure I saw the black cat he cut out of construction paper. But it still didn't seem like Halloween to me, and I said so to Dollie.

"Why don't we get together after supper," she said. "We could tell some ghost stories. Bet that'd do it."

"Yeah," Davis said. "I know a real good one."

I grinned at him. "Don't you have friends waiting with a list of important things to do tonight? You know, outhouses to push over, chickens to steal, trouble to make?"

"Naw, that's kid stuff," he said. "Ghost stories are more fun, especially when they're true."

"You know a true one?" Jacob asked.

"Yeah, but it's too scary for young kids."

Oren frowned. "Who you calling young? Ten's old enough for anything."

Wyatt's eyes widened. "Eight's old enough, isn't it, Davis?"

"Six is, too. Right, Davis?" Ethan asked.

"You'll have to see what Mama says." Davis gave them a serious look. "Ghost stories can be real dangerous. I heard tell of kids your age waking up with snow-white hair after listening to stories as scary as the one I'm gonna tell."

Dollie grinned at me. "Where'll we meet?"

"I know," Jacob said. "Up on the seawall."

Dollie nodded. "See you after supper then."

They waved good-bye and cut across the empty lot to their house.

Jacob raced home and tackled his chores, then fidgeted all through supper. But after we ate, he helped me clean up. He washed while I dried and put everything away. I tried to keep from thinking about the Halloweens I'd spent with Wilma, the cookies, the hot cider, but she was always there in the back of my mind. We loved to tell ghost stories, too, huddled around her potbelly stove.

Light faded till only a soft glow lolled on the horizon. We waited outside under the lean-to, and soon Dollie, Davis, and Oren came running across the lane.

"What happened to Wyatt and Ethan?" I asked.

"Mama said ghost stories would give 'em night-mares," Dollie said. "And thank goodness she did." She blew out a heavy sigh. "It would've been bad enough looking after them up on that seawall, but I sure didn't want to get woke up all the livelong night."

We picked our way up the trail, found a small clearing in the cedars, and sat in a circle, knee to knee, at the edge of the oyster-shell road. The night smelled of seaweed and tarred pilings. I glanced past the harbor to the bay and saw the moon, orange as Wyatt's crayon pumpkin, peeking above the water.

"Who's gonna start?" Dollie asked.

"Sadie can go first," Davis said.

I shook my head. "I'd rather hear yours first."

"Okay. If you're sure."

"Is this the true story?" Oren asked.

"I already told you it was. Now keep your voice down."

"Okay, okay," Oren whispered.

A warm breeze rustled through the cedars, and water lapped against the boats and piers below. I heard Davis draw a deep breath and let it out slow.

"This is the *real* story of the headless horseman," he began. "The *true* story. And it took place fifty years ago not far from this very town." He looked from face to face, his eyes glinting in the moonlight.

"From ranches all along the Nueces River, cattle were disappearing. The ranchers were mad. They called on the sheriff and told him he'd better do something to catch the thieves. So the sheriff deputized thirty men and staked them out with the herds to watch for rustlers.

"Long about midnight of the second night, under a moon just like this one, three of the deputies saw shadowy riders coming over a rise. Five men eased right through the middle of the herd, split half the cattle away from the rest, and started driving them south toward Mexico. The deputies chased after them, and the rustlers took off. When the dust settled, it looked like the thieves had gotten clean away. But one lay shot and left for dead. The deputies brought him into town to be hung for rustling, but he died the next day from his wounds before they could string a rope to the gallows.

"Now this didn't sit too well with the sheriff. He'd been cheated out of his hanging, cheated out of using it to show the rest of those rustlers what gets done to those who steal. That's when he came up with an idea. A brilliant idea—and a horrible one."

"What'd he do?" Oren whispered.

"I'll tell you if you'll be quiet long enough."

"Okay, okay."

"The sheriff," Davis said in a slow and deliberate voice, "did something no one expected. He had the dead rustler's head cut off. He tied the man's body to his saddle. And then he tied the head, hat and all, to the saddle horn."

Dollie gasped. "You're making this up, Davis Gillem."

He shook his head. "No, I'm not. It's true history. Gunther heard it from his daddy, who heard it from Spits Cameron, and he's a deacon over at the Methodist church. It's true all right."

"What happened next?" Jacob asked.

"Well, the sheriff slapped that horse on the rump, that's what happened. Sent that headless rustler riding through the valley as a warning to the rest of his gang." Davis dropped his voice to a whisper. "And now, people say he can still be seen riding with his head on his saddle horn, especially on nights like this when the moon is full."

I glanced at the moon and shivered in the warm breeze.

"He rides the valleys and all through the towns," Davis said. "Some say he rides as a warning to thieves to change their wicked ways. And some say he rides after all righteous men, vengeful for the bloody thing they done to him."

"Well, which is it?" Oren whispered. "Is he after bad men or good men?"

"He must've been a real mad rustler," Jacob said.

Davis smiled, and his teeth gleamed in the bright moonlight. He turned to me. "Now it's your turn, Sadie."

I laughed and shook my head. "I don't think I can beat that one."

"Aw, sure you can," Oren said.

"My ghost story's a bit different. It happened a little over a year ago, but it's true."

"You mean you saw a real ghost and you didn't tell me?" Jacob asked.

"Girls don't tell brothers everything, Jacob. Besides, it happened to Wilma's brother back in Missouri, not to me."

"Oh."

"Who's Wilma?" Dollie asked.

Her question caught me off guard. "Um . . . no one, really."

"Sadie's best friend," Jacob said.

A cloud passed over the moon, and Dollie's eyes disappeared under its shadow. After a moment, I heard her say, "Oh."

Davis shifted, rattling bits of oyster shell. "Go ahead," he said. "Let's hear it."

The cloud moved on, leaving moonlight to brighten cheeks and glitter in eyes. Relieved, I began.

"Well, Jack is Wilma's oldest brother," I explained. "He and his wife, Faye Jean, used to live in an old house not far from us with their three kids." I reached into my memory and saw Wilma all over again, breathless and wide-eyed, telling me the story in whispers like she was scared the ghost might hear and pop up right in front of her.

"One summer night, while Jack was drifting off to sleep, he heard footsteps in his house. He thought it was one of the kids, but when he looked in on them, they were sound asleep. He checked the house, and when he didn't find anything unusual, he figured he must've dreamed it all.

"The next night, he heard the footsteps again. But this time they came into his room and stopped at the foot of his bed. Moonlight streamed through his bedroom window, bright enough to see most anything. Trouble was, there was nothing there to see. While he stared at the foot of his bed, thinking he might be dreaming again, he heard a match strike. He even smelled sulfur, but he saw no flame. Then came the smell of tobacco smoke, drifting across his bed.

"Quick as a shot he was up, lighting the lamp. Faye Jean hadn't heard a thing, but she pulled the sheet up to her chin and waited for Jack to check the house. When he came back to bed, he still had no answers for what he'd heard.

"The next night, Jack went to the outhouse before going to bed. Soon as he got inside good, he heard the wood floor creak behind him. Now wood floors pop and creak all the time, even in outhouses, so those sounds didn't make him all that suspicious. Not at first, anyway. It wasn't till he felt something move up close to his back that he got scared."

"How'd he know it was there?" Jacob asked.

"'Cause on this hot summer night, he felt his back go ice cold."

I heard Dollie suck in a breath, and goose bumps popped out all over my arms. This story always did give me the willies, even when I told it.

"Well, the hair on the back of Jack's neck stood straight up and gooseflesh rippled across his scalp. He whirled around to see what was behind him, but like before, nothing was there."

"Jeepers," Oren whispered. "What'd he do then?"

"He ran back to the house where he sat up all night, too scared to go to sleep, and for sure, too scared to go to the outhouse again.

"But by the next morning, Jack was getting mad. He didn't like the idea of living the rest of his life chasing footsteps and watching his back, so he decided he'd have to talk to that ghost."

"Can you do that?" Oren asked. "Talk to ghosts, I mean?"

"Oren," Davis whispered through his teeth, "hush and let her tell the story."

"Well, that night when Faye Jean finally drifted off to sleep, Jack sat up again, waiting for the ghost to come back."

"And did it?" asked Dollie.

I nodded. "Just like before. Footsteps sounded through the house and came to a stop at the foot of his bed. Jack waited, and sure enough, he heard a match being struck. He smelled sulfur and tobacco smoke. Then, in a low voice so as not to wake Faye Jean, Jack said, 'There ain't nobody here for you, Mr. Ghost. You need to go find your own folks and let us be.'"

"Then what happened?" Oren asked.

"Well, that tobacco smoke just faded away."

"You mean the ghost left?" Dollie asked.

"Appeared so. But the whole affair upset poor Jack so much he couldn't abide the smell of tobacco after that and had to give up smoking."

"Where do you think that ghost went?" Oren asked.

"Off to haunt someone else," Davis said. "That's what ghosts do."

"I've smelled tobacco smoke at night lots of times," Jacob whispered. "You don't think that ghost could've followed us here, do you?"

"That was no ghost, Jacob. That was Daddy." I let out a laugh, but even I could hear the uneasiness in it.

"But I heard tell of ghosts doing things like that," Davis said.

I shuddered. "We do *not* have a ghost in our house, Davis."

"Maybe not, but—"

"Sssssh."

I looked at Dollie. She held a finger to her lips. "I heard something," she whispered.

I froze and listened.

Wind sighed through the cedars. Boats jerked against mooring lines. Water thumped under bows. Then I heard it.

The striking of a match.

Oren's eyes popped wide as a hoot owl's. When the smell of sulfur hit, he let out a sound so awful it pierced right through me. In seconds he was on his feet, thrashing down the seawall with Jacob at his heels.

"I'm going, too," Dollie said, jumping up.

Davis laughed. "Come on," he said, reaching for my hand. "Our audience is deserting."

He helped me up, then pulled back like he was embarrassed at the free way he'd grabbed my hand. He nodded toward the trail. "After you."

We scrambled down the dark trail, and when we got to the lean-to, we found Jacob and Oren huddled under Mr. Winslow's rickety table.

Davis doubled over laughing.

"Stop it," Dollie hissed. "I really did hear something. You heard it, too, didn't you, Sadie?"

I nodded, still a bit shaky. "A match striking."

"How could we hear such a thing?" Dollie asked. "There wasn't a soul around."

"Aw, someone on the harbor road lit up a smoke and the wind carried it," Davis said. "The smell, too. Had to be."

Dollie gave him a skeptical look. "I didn't see anyone."

Oren crawled out from under the table. "Well, I've had enough ghost stories for this Halloween. I'm going to bed."

Jacob's head bobbed. "Me too."

Davis laughed again, but when he looked at me, I was surprised to see admiration in his eyes. "That was some story, Sadie. I don't think I've ever heard the likes before."

Dollie nodded. "But if you tell it again next year,

we're gonna have to pick another place. That sea-wall is way too spooky at night."

I laughed, too, but I was still bewildered about what we'd heard. I eased closer to our door and watched Dollie and Davis start across the lane.

"See you tomorrow," Davis called over his shoulder.

I waved. "Tomorrow."

That night the wind died, and heat gathered against the ceiling like something alive and breathing. I threw the sheet off me and wondered if Davis had been right about someone on the harbor road striking that match. It did make sense. But considering the way that sound came at just the right moment, I also had to wonder if my story hadn't somehow conjured up the real ghost—Jack's ghost. Davis said he'd heard tell of spirits doing things like that.

Sticky with sweat, I scooted closer to the window screen and thought about the way Davis had looked at me. It reminded me of the way Daddy sometimes looked at Mama. Like she was smart. Like she was special.

I wished I could talk to Wilma about all this.

Chapter Nineteen

AFTER A SWEATY NIGHT, I passed through the cannery doors the next morning thankful to be working in a room full of icy shrimp. But by the time I peeled my bucket of shrimp and left for home, the sun was up and the steamy heat was, too.

Halfway to school, my chest felt like I'd been breathing water. I remembered the stillness before the hurricane and glanced over my shoulder to check the southern horizon. The sky shone clear blue. But to the north, deep color had crept above the tree line. I watched the blue-gray widen, watched it darken and tinge green. I'd seen storms in Missouri—bad ones with tornadoes—move that quick. They'd sweep in, uprooting trees, whipping roofs off barns and houses. You hardly had time to run for the root cellar. I looked around me. No one had a cellar on these flats, and no one was running. Fear gripped my throat so tight all I could do was nudge Dollie and point to the sky.

"Hey," she said. "We got us a norther coming."

Davis let out a happy whoop and I stared at them both. "A norther?"

"Yeah," Davis said. "It'll cool things off real quick."

Within minutes half the sky had clouded over, and the heavy curtain of warm air shifted. It swirled around my bare legs and billowed my skirt. Then a cool gust hit, drying my sweaty skin and pasting my dress against my body. The wind smelled sweet and clean, like the good Lord had scooped up all the air over His forests and lakes and blew it our way.

"We'd better hurry!" Dollie hollered. "It might rain."

She grabbed Ethan's hand, and Davis took Wyatt's. Jacob and Oren were ahead of us as usual. We ran the last two blocks to school and scooted through the doors.

But it didn't rain. The skies cleared, and the temperature stayed nice all day. "Sixty-eight degrees," Mrs. Doogan said, looking at the class thermometer. "Now that's much better."

It *was* better, but the cool, dry norther seemed to stir something odd in the kids. They seemed rowdy and fearless, like something magical had swept in and made all things possible. They acted like they could do anything they wanted and never have to answer for it. Claudia must've felt it, too, because she was more annoying than ever. I found myself wishing I could teach her a lesson in manners. I might've, too, but I couldn't think of a thing that would get through that thick head of hers. She'd already made up her mind she was better than everyone else, and nothing could change that.

When the last bell rang, kids burst through doors, whooping like they'd been let out of prison. Excitement crackled through the halls. We rounded up Ethan and Wyatt, met Davis outside, and stood around waiting for Jacob and Oren. They were usually the first ones out of the building. When crowds thinned and teachers began to leave, I got worried. Davis left to check the boys' fifth-grade classroom and came back running.

"I saw them from a second-floor window," he said, pointing toward the Jackson Hotel. "This way."

I hurried down the sidewalk after him and saw a circle of boys across the road from the hotel, jeering and shouting. "What's happening?" I called.

"Fight!" Davis hollered over his shoulder.

I squeezed between the cheering kids and saw

Jacob, lip bloodied, pinned to the ground by a big boy in khaki pants and new shoes.

"Hit 'im again, Harold," a kid called from the circle.

But Jacob heaved Harold to the side and swung a fist into his face. It landed below the kid's eye and left a gash.

Oren laughed. "I knew you could do it!"

I shoved him out of the way, leaped into the circle, and grabbed Jacob's arm. "Stop it! Stop it now!" I pulled hard and saw Davis towering over Harold. He had a tight grip on the boy's collar.

The crowd backed away, and I yanked Jacob to the sidewalk. Breathless, I pointed to his lip. "Look at you. What are you going to tell Daddy?" I jerked at his torn sleeve. "And what's Mama gonna say when she sees this shirt?"

Jacob ignored me, glaring over my shoulder at Harold. I turned to see Davis twist the boy's arm behind his back, holding him secure while he talked to a younger kid close by. I listened but couldn't make out what they were saying. When Davis finished he gave Harold a push and watched till the boy shuffled off.

I gripped Jacob's arm. "What happened?"

"Nothing," he said, jerking away.

Davis pulled a frayed handkerchief from his back pocket. "I'll tell you what happened." His voice sounded thick and tight. He dabbed at Jacob's bloodied lip. "The kid called him a bay rat. Told him to stay on his side of the tracks with the rest of the bay trash where he belonged."

I stared at Davis, wondering what could make a kid say such a thing. Maybe Jacob did something, made him mad. But all the way home, I thought about Claudia and her friends, remembering the way they never missed a chance to laugh at me. Maybe Jacob hadn't done anything at all.

I put one foot down in front of the other and finally reached our lane. I guess I dreaded going home almost as much as Jacob did. I didn't want to see Mama's and Daddy's faces when they learned what some of the town kids thought of us. They deserved better. We all did.

But Daddy sent me outside with the kids when he talked to Jacob, so I didn't get to see how they took the news. That evening, after we climbed into our loft, Mama opened her Bible. She ran a finger down a page and stopped on a verse.

"A soft answer turneth away wrath," she read, "but grievous words stir up anger." She eased the book closed. "Proverbs fifteen, verse one," she said, and blew out the lamp.

That night, the first cool night we'd had in this place, I curled up under Mama's quilt and thought about that verse. I wanted to believe I'd be strong enough to handle meanness with a soft answer the way the Bible wanted me to. But as I stared into the darkness, waiting for sleep, I knew in my heart I'd fail. Just like Jacob.

Chapter Twenty

COLD, CRISP AIR MET ME when I left for the cannery the next morning. The bay had glassed over, reflecting a sky so thick with stars you could hardly see black between them. The nice weather appeared to have the same effect on grown-ups as it did on the kids at school yesterday. Steps quickened and so did words. Laughter cut through the early stillness and echoed across the harbor.

When we reached the cannery, I pushed through the double doors and started right in on my bucket of shrimp. But something bristled in the air, something I hadn't felt before, and soon a squabble broke out between two women working at the table behind me. Cross whispers turned to loud, angry words, and we finally stopped working to watch.

"You're not fooling anyone," Margie said, her face pinched and red. "Sidling up to my Otis, all fluttery and helpless." She huffed and tossed a smirking grin at Selma, the short blond woman next to her. "He knows exactly what you are."

Selma slapped her unpeeled shrimp onto the table and turned with a daring glare. "Listen, honey, I don't do anything I'm not invited to do."

Margie blinked. Then she grabbed her half-filled bucket and flung wet shrimp all over Selma. The splatter peppered my face and hair, and the next thing I knew, the two women hit the floor in a tangle of legs and fists.

Two cannery bosses pulled them apart and shoved them toward the door. With their hair snarled, clothes twisted and smeared with shrimp juice, they left. I saw grins all around when we turned back to our work, but I knew if Mama got wind of this, she might change her mind about my working in such a place.

I peeled my bucket of shrimp and got home quick as I could. I'd wasted time watching the fight, and I still had to help with the chores. But what worried me most was having enough time to wash up proper. Those crazy women had flung shrimp juice all over me, even in my hair.

I scrubbed and changed clothes, but there wasn't enough water drawn to wash my hair. Mama had a keen nose, though. If I smelled of shrimp, she'd never let me out the door. When she didn't say anything, I raced off, relieved.

On the way to school, I wondered how things would go for Jacob when everyone saw his swollen lip. I was sure Harold would be sporting a black eye along with his cut cheekbone, and sure, too, that by dinnertime, everyone would know what had happened.

We had to hurry to make the bell. I slid into my desk and watched to see if news of Jacob's fight had reached my seventh-grade class, but all was quiet. It wasn't until Mrs. Doogan passed out our history test that I heard a soft ripple of laughter. I looked up to see a dozen smirking faces turned in my direction. I ducked my head and stared at my test paper. The kids knew. The next time I heard snickers I kept my eyes on my work.

The dinner bell finally rang, and I hung back to talk to Dollie in the hall. "Did you hear the laughing?" I asked. "They know about the fight."

Dollie frowned. "They weren't laughing about the fight, Sadie."

"What then?"

"They were laughing at Claudia, behind you."

"Perfect Claudia?" I grinned at the thought. "What did she do?"

Dollie glanced at her feet and looked back at me. "Claudia pointed at you and held her nose."

I slid a hand over my unwashed hair.

"Come on," she said, pulling me toward the door. "Let's get out of this hall before we get into trouble. We'll talk while we eat."

From the hallway, I saw Claudia and her friends sitting on the cement steps. I stopped, sure my heart would skip right out my chest, but Dollie pushed me on.

"Keep walking and don't look back," she said.

I let her pull me through the middle of them. We stepped around skirts and sandwiches, and just as we cleared the last of it, I heard one of the girls say, "What *is* that awful smell?"

I stopped, my back to them, but Dollie gave my arm a jerk and kept me walking.

"Don't you know?" another asked.

I stopped again. This voice I recognized. Claudia's words rang across half the playground, and kids from first grade up turned to see what was happening. Out of the growing sea of faces, I saw Gunther and Davis frown.

Dollie tugged at me again, but this time I refused to budge. With my back still turned to Claudia, I waited for her to finish. She didn't shout this time,

< 179 >

though. She whispered, and the girls beside her howled with laughter.

Whisper or shout didn't matter to me. The sound of that laughter twisted so tight inside me I could hardly breathe. The ugly misery I'd been feeling since that first day at school reared up, all teeth and claws, so powerful I feared it might shred every last good thing in me. I shuddered. I wanted to tear into those girls. Make them hurt. The way Jacob hurt. The way they were hurting me.

Fists clenched, I whirled around, and with satisfaction, I saw their silly grins disappear. The girls stared wide-eyed at my reaction. I stepped toward them, saw them flinch, and felt someone grab my arm. Dollie and Davis pulled me around, and when I turned, I saw tall Gunther there, too. He whispered something to Davis and strode off toward the girls.

Dollie and Davis pulled me away and headed to the farthermost corner of the playground. Still holding my arm, Davis eased me to the ground under a stand of skinny oaks and plopped down hard beside me. "Stupid Claudia," he muttered. He scooted close till we were shoulder to shoulder.

"Don't worry, Sadie," Dollie said, sitting on the other side of me. "It's not that bad. Everyone knows Claudia jumps at any chance to embarrass people like us."

I stared at her. Not that bad? My eyes burned, and my teeth clamped so tight my jaw throbbed. I turned on her.

"What do you know?" I demanded. "People like *us*?" I sucked in a breath and flung my bitterness at her. "I'm nothing like you, Dollie. Nothing! Just look at you." I spit the words at her. "You're the bay rat, not me."

I threw my dinner sack in the dirt, scrambled to my feet, and turned on her again. "I had a good life before we came to this . . . this awful place with its ugly tar-paper houses and hateful name-calling." My chest heaved. "I came from better. I had a home—a nice home, Dollie. With real walls. And floors. And . . . and nice furniture. And a porch swing . . . and . . . and . . ."

I stood there with my mouth open, all out of words, tears dripping from my chin.

Dollie wiped at the wetness on her cheek with the back of her hand and stared past me. "We had a nice home once, too," she said. "Just like yours."

Her words knocked the wind out of me. Like the time I fell from the tiptop of our big sycamore tree back home and hit the ground so hard I thought I'd die. Only this time, watching Dollie and Davis walk away, I knew I'd die for sure.

Chapter Twenty-One

I LIED TO MAMA. I walked right off that playground, went home, and told her I was sick.

I guess it wasn't all a lie. With Wilma gone, and now Dollie and Davis, too, I never felt so sick in my whole life. It must've shown 'cause Mama gave me a quick glance and put me straight to bed. I was grateful. But the longer I lay there, the clearer I saw things, and the worse I felt about what I'd done.

If I'd only listened.

I'd been so busy blaming Mama and Daddy for bringing us to this place, I never considered that the Gillems might've come here the same way we did. I remembered, then, what Dollie had told me that night in the cotton fields. She'd said her family had to leave Ohio to find work. I had to wonder how many others down our lane had been forced out of jobs and homes and into these tents and tar-paper shacks. Or cardboard boxes.

The Gillems, the Wallers, the Mulgroves—maybe all of them suffered. Those people we saw on the road to Texas must've suffered, too, and we weren't different from any of them. We flitted from camp to camp like birds making our way south, same as everybody.

Truth was, the Depression had turned us all into Mr. Sparrows. I could see that, now.

Mama climbed the loft ladder to bring me a cup of potato soup. I hated that I'd made her worry, but I couldn't eat. She frowned and ran a cool hand across my cheek and forehead.

"I'm okay, Mama," I told her.

She patted my arm and took the cup down with her, but I knew she still worried. I did, too. I worried that I'd never get a chance to make up for what I'd said to Dollie. Over and over, I recalled my words to her. Words so mean and spiteful, I feared we'd both carry the weight of them around with us the rest of our days. But most grievous of all was remembering the hurt on Dollie's face. I'd let my sour feelings about leaving home keep me from seeing any good in this place. And I'd used Dollie's friendship to ease my loneliness without giving even a portion of it back to her.

I'd done those awful things. And now I had to find a way to undo them.

When Jacob came home he gave me a knowing look. He knew I wasn't really sick, but he didn't tell on me. In fact, he waved at me before he took off to fill the water buckets. After what he'd been through with Harold, I guess he understood about Claudia. But I was sure Dollie and Davis hadn't said anything to him about what happened later. He might not have been so friendly if they had.

I didn't sleep much that night, but when I did, I dreamed about Wilma, about that last day beside the river and the promise I'd given her. I saw the pain in her blue eyes all over again, clear as day. Then Wilma changed, and it was Dollie I saw. It was Dollie's eyes that were full of sorrow.

I woke up long before the whistle, so full of grief my chest ached. I still didn't know what to do with my promise, but I knew I couldn't hurt Dollie again because of it. With no way to give Wilma my friendship anymore, all I could do now was ask God to take care of her and help her find a new best friend, someone as good as Dollie had already been to me.

< 184 >

When the whistle blew, I pretended to be asleep and Mama didn't try to wake me. I couldn't bear the thought of facing Davis at the cannery. Mr. Gillem, either. I'd betrayed them both by acting like I was better.

Before breakfast, Mama looked in on me. I told her I was fine and I'd be going to school. I couldn't bring myself to lie to her again, even if it meant facing what I'd done.

"We've got some of Mr. Caughlin's big brown eggs this morning," she said, smiling at me. "Get dressed and I'll make you a good breakfast."

I washed up, braided my hair, and put on my morning-glory dress, but I still couldn't eat. I kept thinking about what was waiting for me on the other side of that door. I gave my egg to Jacob when Mama wasn't looking. He wolfed it down and ran off— to find Oren, I supposed. But a few minutes later, he burst back through the door.

"I told Oren I'd be walking with you today," he said. He caught Mama's puzzled look and added, "Since you're feeling poorly, that is."

I nodded, managed a grateful smile, and followed Jacob outside. I looked for Dollie and Davis, but I knew they hadn't waited. I spotted them far down the road, walking with Wyatt and Ethan. They paused, waited for Oren to catch up, then continued on without us.

Mama had been right. Who you are inside always shows. It finally showed clear enough for me to see, and yesterday, Dollie and Davis saw it, too. I set off down the road, knowing this would be the longest day of my life. I didn't like what I'd become, but with each step, I grew more determined to find a way to change.

When I got to class, Dollie was already seated. Just seeing her sitting there, not looking at me, not smiling, made my heart ache. She never looked my way once, but most everyone else did. I expected it. I expected the hateful look I got from Claudia, too, but Gunther's smile surprised me. My recollection of him yesterday was fuzzy, but I was almost certain he'd been at Davis's side, helping me. He'd never been friendly with me before, and it puzzled me a bit—him being a town kid and all. I stared at him, wishing I could remember more.

Claudia started up the aisle in her new autumn-colored dress, and Gunther pulled in his long leg so she could saunter by. She tossed him her classic glare—which Gunther ignored—smiled sweetly at Mrs. Doogan, and sharpened her pencil. When Claudia turned around she looked right at me, something she never did in the classroom. I couldn't help but wonder what she was up to, but it didn't take long to find out. With Mrs. Doogan's desk safely behind her, Claudia's lips curled in a nasty little grin, her eyes crossed, and out popped her tongue.

Snickers rippled around the room. I tossed a quick glance at Dollie and caught a stricken look on her face.

Claudia moved slowly down the aisle, making sure everyone saw her. Her tongue stuck out so far, I wished she'd trip over it.

Then she did! Only it wasn't her tongue she tripped over; it was Gunther's foot. She plunged forward, her eyes big as goose eggs, and the next second she was face down on the floor beside me.

Gasps hissed around the room and quickly turned to laughter. Mrs. Doogan banged her ruler on her desk. "Quiet!" she shouted.

Claudia scrambled to her feet. "You idiot!" she screamed at Gunther. She brushed furiously at her dress. "You did that on purpose!"

Gunther unfolded his legs and stood up. "I'm so sorry, Claudia," he said, oozing sincerity. He turned to Mrs. Doogan with a shrug. "It's these long legs of mine. I can't seem to keep them out of the way."

Claudia shoved him, and he fell back onto his seat. "Shut up, you moron!"

The class roared. She whirled around and stomped her foot at them. "I said shut up!"

"Claudia!" Mrs. Doogan's ruler sounded again, louder this time. "No more outbursts."

Behind Claudia's back, Gunther turned and winked at me.

I stared at him in disbelief.

"But, Mrs. Doogan," Claudia sputtered. "Didn't you see him? He deliberately stuck his leg in the aisle. He should be suspended. He should be expelled. He should be—"

"Clau-di-a!"

Claudia's mouth clamped shut. The shuffling of feet and limbs turning to attention whooshed across the room.

While everyone faced forward, waiting to see what Mrs. Doogan would do, I stole another look at Gunther. Had he really tripped her on purpose? He sat straight in his seat, shoulders back, shining with innocence.

Mrs. Doogan's chair scraped across the floor. She stood.

"Now," she said, her eyes narrowing at Claudia. "Since you've chosen to make the class participate in this event, please advise us of your condition."

Claudia blinked.

"Are you hurt?" asked Mrs. Doogan.

Claudia swelled, opened her mouth, then closed it again. Her jaw tightened. "No, ma'am," she said.

"And did you receive an apology for this incident?"

Her face turned an angry red. "Yes, ma'am," she whispered.

"Good," said Mrs. Doogan. "Then I will return to my work, and I suggest you do the same." She scanned the class. "All of you."

When Claudia turned, she gave me a look mean enough to sink a shrimp boat and slid into the seat behind me.

"And, Gunther," Mrs. Doogan called.

He jerked his long legs under his desk. "Yes, ma'am?"

"I trust you've gained control of your limbs?"

"Yes, ma'am." He gave a reassuring nod, but when Mrs. Doogan looked away, he turned and grinned at me again.

I was sure now. Gunther had found a way to embarrass Claudia in front of the whole class, just like she'd done to me.

Claudia had been bested.

A flood of satisfaction hit me. After all, it was only fitting that she got a taste of her own meanness. Like Mama always said, you reap what you sow. "Careful," she'd warn us. "You get back what you send out into this world."

Claudia had done a good job of proving that today. I leaned back, enjoying the moment till I

< 189 >

caught Dollie's eye. Just seeing her made me flinch. I guess I'd been busy proving Mama's favorite Bible verse, too. I'd certainly reaped some of the misery my hateful words had sown.

But Mama was also fond of saying, "A body can sow joy just as easy as sorrow." That little thought stayed with me all through Mrs. Doogan's discussion of cumulus, cirrus, and stratus clouds.

Sow joy. Reap joy.

By the time we'd moved on to history, I'd decided Mama could be right. It made perfect sense. If I sowed joy, then the joy I got back might be Dollie. Pleased with my conclusion, I smiled right in the middle of Mrs. Doogan's discussion of the Boston Tea Party. How hard could this be? I *wanted* to be a better person, a better friend.

But the more I thought about it, the more I realized where Mama's Bible verse was leading me. Joy was simple, but if I wanted to reap forgiveness—*Dollie's* forgiveness—would I have to sow forgiveness?

An uneasiness jiggled in the pit of my stomach.

I'd have to forgive someone.

I cringed, remembering Claudia's nasty laughter. Would I have to forgive Claudia—mean Claudia— if I wanted Dollie to forgive me?

I flashed back to the many times Claudia had made fun of me, to the nasty look she'd just given me before Gunther tripped her. Was I supposed to for-give that? The loathsome thought bounced around in my head till I couldn't stand it another minute.

No. Uh-uh. I couldn't possibly. I'd rather eat worms. Besides, Claudia didn't deserve forgiveness. She set herself above all the kids from our side of town. She treated us like we were nothing—like *I* was nothing. Like . . .

I shot a horrified glance at Dollie, and the awful words I'd said yesterday rushed back at me.

I'd treated Dollie like she was nothing. I'd even called her a bay rat.

I shuddered.

Truth hit me hard and cold, like the icy drenching I got when I fell into the river last winter. I was no better than Claudia.

How could Dollie ever forgive me?

Chapter Twenty-Two

I QUIT WORKING at the cannery. Shame played a big part in my decision, but more than that, it finally became clear to me that no amount of money would change a thing. I'd still be Sadie, inside and out, Missouri or Texas, this side of the tracks or the other. I didn't know how to be anything else.

Jacob went back to walking with Oren to school. I expected it and didn't mind, though I envied him having a best friend. I missed Dollie.

When he left, I hung back, letting everyone get down the road a piece before I started off to school. After a few days I could tell Mama had questions, but she didn't ask them. I got hugs, instead, like somehow she knew I needed them.

I don't know what went on between Gunther and Claudia, but she seemed to be a bit more mindful of the humiliation she doled out. Even so, I still couldn't forgive her. And I couldn't bring myself to face Dollie yet, either.

November weather changed so fast, from hot to cold and back again, that I hardly knew what to wear in the mornings. In town, store owners painted bright pictures on their windows of turkeys and corn and pumpkins, preparing for the coming holiday.

Duck season would open on Thursday, November 16, just one week before Thanksgiving. I knew Daddy would be itching to bring in his limit, and sure enough, on the evening of the fifteenth, he polished off his bowl of oyster stew and sent Jacob for the shotgun.

"Season opens tomorrow," he told Mama. "Me and Dan are going."

Jacob handed Daddy the gun, careful to keep the barrel pointed down like he was taught.

"We'll be taking Jacob and Oren with us to do the retrieving," Daddy said.

Jacob flashed a grin, but Mama frowned. "Tomorrow's Thursday, John. They've got school."

Daddy didn't look pleased about us missing school,

but he shook his head. "We don't keep them out for foolish things, Raine. Missing a day to put meat on the table won't hurt 'em, smart as they are."

Mama sighed. "Then Sadie will have to stay home, too, to help with the canning."

Daddy gave her a bleak nod. "I suppose."

While he cleaned his gun, he fussed about the bag limit being cut from fifteen to twelve. "But with Jacob and Oren along to do the retrieving," he said, "we can bring in enough for four men. That means two dozen for us. You got enough jars and lids?"

Mama nodded. "We got plenty." She called to Jacob. "You'd better top off the water barrel for tomorrow," she told him. "It takes a lot of water to clean ducks."

Early the next morning, the men rowed to the blinds. As soon as it was light, I heard shots popping in the distance and figured Daddy would be bringing home his limit in no time.

That's when Mama told me to run and tell Mrs. Gillem that she was welcome to clean her ducks with us. "Might as well keep the mess in one place," she said.

I looked out the window toward their house, wondering if Mrs. Gillem had kept Dollie home, too.

< 194 >

"Go on," Mama said.

I guess I dragged my feet a bit. I'd let two whole weeks go by without apologizing, and I didn't know what I'd do if Dollie opened the door.

I knocked and stood back, hardly breathing. When Mrs. Gillem answered I saw Dollie sitting behind her at the table, holding baby Caleb. She glanced at me, and my heart skipped.

Maybe this would be the day. Maybe I'd finally find the courage to tell her how foolish I'd been and ask her if we could be friends again.

I spit out Mama's message as best as I could and ran home.

While me and Mama waited for the men to get back, I scrubbed the outside table with lye soap and pulled out the dishpan and washtubs. I set up the extra camp stove for Mrs. Gillem to use, the one Mr. Winslow left, and all the while I thought about Dollie.

A few hours later, I spotted Jacob and Oren, soaked and dragging tow sacks down the seawall. Mama told Oren to leave his by the washtub and run and tell his mama they were back.

"But we can't stay, Mama," Jacob said. "Mr. Gillem says ducks are too plentiful to call it quits just yet. He said we're gonna get our limit twice today."

Jacob didn't seem at all bothered by his wet pants. Laughing, he grabbed a leftover biscuit and stuffed half of it in his mouth.

"You and Mrs. Gillem," he sputtered around the biscuit, "are gonna have forty-eight ducks apiece to can, Mama. Ain't that something?"

Mama frowned. I knew she didn't like the idea of Daddy breaking the hunting rules, and I figured she'd say something for sure. But all that came out of her was, "Don't talk with your mouth full, Jacob. And don't use 'ain't.'"

Jacob dropped the grin and swallowed hard. "Yes, ma'am," he said.

When Oren got back, the boys took off up the trail. "We'll be home soon," Jacob hollered over his shoulder.

I saw Mrs. Gillem walking across the lane with Caleb and three-year-old Tanner. Wyatt and Ethan followed, carrying a washtub between them. Dollie brought up the rear with her mama's pressure cooker hugged tight against her belly. I didn't see Davis, but I wasn't brave enough to ask after him.

Mama and Mrs. Gillem sat on upturned buckets by the tubs, and all us kids gathered on the ground, ready to help with the plucking. Except for Bobby and Tanner, who complained loudly that they wanted something fun to do, too.

I laughed. I hated cleaning ducks, and by the look on Mama's face when she pulled the first one out of the sack, I figured she felt the same way. Seemed to me there wasn't much in this world that could rival the stink of duck innards and singed feathers, not even a mad polecat. But the work had to be done, so I sat between Emily and Ethan and plucked brown, white, and green feathers into the tub.

Over the next hour, we held ducks over a low flame, singed them, and wiped them down with clean rags. Then we gutted them and washed them in fresh water.

While I boiled canning jars and lids, I wondered if I'd ever get a chance to be alone with Dollie. Every once in a while, I'd glance at her, but I never caught her looking my way. After a while, I had to face the fact that she might not want to hear how sorry I was.

About the time Mama had her first seven jars in the pressure cooker, we saw Oren and Jacob coming down the seawall with two more sacks of ducks. Daddy and Mr. Gillem followed close behind.

"Bagged our limit," Daddy said, grinning.

"Twice!" Mr. Gillem said. "Whaddaya think of that, Irene?" He laughed, grabbed Mrs. Gillem, and waltzed her around a few steps. Everyone giggled, even Dollie.

Fussing, hands flapping in the air, Mrs. Gillem told him, "Stop acting the fool," but she had a big grin on her face when she said it.

"We'll go back early Thanksgiving morning," Mr. Gillem said, "so we can have fresh duck and oyster stuffing for our dinner."

"As long as you do the cleaning next time," Mrs. Gillem told him.

Mama agreed. And then she invited them to have their holiday dinner with us, right there under the lean-to.

"We've got a lot to be thankful for," Daddy said. "Not the least of which is good friends."

Mr. Gillem leaned down to shake Daddy's hand. "Good friends, indeed," he said.

I glanced at Dollie, but she'd already looked away.

With another four dozen ducks waiting, we had to get busy. Us kids helped the men clean the second round and left Mama and Mrs. Gillem free to do the canning. Their pressure cookers would steam well into the evening, but we knew there wouldn't be enough hours in the day to do all those ducks. That second round would have to go into the icebox for tomorrow. By dark, our two families would have twenty-one quarts of canned meat apiece and that much more in the icebox for canning tomorrow.

Daddy sent Jacob and Oren to Grobe's Grocery for ice. Stick candy, too, a reward for our help. I spotted the boys about fifteen minutes later coming across the road, their pants wet, fingers tucked into string-tied blocks of melting ice. They listed to one side to keep balanced under their heavy loads. Red, yellow, and purple stick candy bulged from Oren's shirt pocket.

Mama added potatoes to the pot of thick duck stew simmering on the stove and eased herself onto our rickety bench. Daddy gave her a questioning look. Her face had turned pale as cream gravy, and her ankles looked like tree stumps.

I dragged the rocking chair out of the house. "Come sit here, Mama," I said, "and lean back awhile." I slipped a pillow behind her back and lifted her swollen feet onto an upturned bucket. "Can I get you some cool water?"

She patted my hand. "That'd be good, Sadie."

"And don't worry about finishing up supper," I added. "I can do it."

Mama smiled and leaned back. She looked worn thin, light as the pages of her Bible, like she'd blow away with the breeze if it weren't for the baby she carried inside her. I ladled water into a cup and took it to her, but her eyes had already closed.

< 199 >

"Don't worry too much, Sadie," Mrs. Gillem whispered. "It's the baby. The last month or so can be hard on a body."

I nodded, sat the cup on the bench close to Mama, and busied myself pouring flour into Mama's big mixing bowl. When I turned, I glimpsed Dollie looking at me for the first time today. She didn't smile, but she didn't look away, either. Fear and hope twined so tight in my chest I couldn't tell which I felt most. But I'd been forced to give up on the idea of getting her alone. Everything I wanted to say to her would have to wait.

I made four dozen biscuits, and Mrs. Gillem sent Dollie over to their house to help get them all baked. When we'd finished with supper and the dishes were washed, I packed up the leftovers. "For Davis," I told Mrs. Gillem. "He'll probably be hungry when he gets in."

She thanked me, and after they'd all gone home, Jacob pulled Mama's chair into the house. She sat back down, and we washed up for bed.

I thought Daddy would be too tired to read, but he lit the lantern and opened *The Last of the Mohicans* to chapter seven. I peeled the paper off the last two inches of my purple-striped stick candy and sucked on the end till it was pointed as a newly sharpened pencil.

About the time the Iroquois attacked Hawkeye

and his party, I glanced at Mama. She'd fallen asleep in her rocking chair, her swollen feet propped on the bench and her arms folded limp across her belly.

I woke up the next morning to pale lamplight and knew Mama must be starting Daddy's breakfast. I looked over the edge of the loft and saw her hobble across the chilly pine floor on her swollen feet. "Mama," I whispered. "You need to go back to bed." I threw back my covers and scrambled down the ladder in my nightgown. "I can make breakfast for Daddy this morning."

It took some talking. Mama's stubborn about getting meals for her family, but I finally convinced her to stay off her feet a while longer.

Before the four o'clock whistle sounded, I had biscuits in the oven and thin slices of duck breast floured and sizzling in the skillet. While Daddy ate, I talked to him about letting me stay home from school. "Mama's going to need some help with the canning," I reminded him.

He looked relieved, and agreed to let me stay home. Still, when Aubrey showed up, Daddy hesitated at the door.

"I won't let her do much," I assured him. "I've helped Mama lots of times, Daddy. I can handle the pressure cooker."

He nodded and finally smiled at me. "You're a pretty smart girl, all right." He slid his black cap over his head and swung himself out the door.

After I fed the kids and got Jacob off to school, I pulled the rocking chair outside for Mama and started jars to boiling. She was antsy about sitting idle with so much work to be done, but I told her this was the perfect time for me to try canning on my own.

She finally leaned back, but from her chair, she watched every move I made. She told me the best way to get fresh meat into the jars, reminded me to wipe the rims, and made sure I kept the pressure gauge steady at ten pounds.

I did everything she said, and while I watched the gauge, she told me stories about helping her mother put up preserves, and how Grandma liked to play hide-and-seek at twilight like she was one of the kids. "But your grandma would always giggle," Mama said, "and give away her hiding place."

Then Mama told me about the time she almost drowned swimming in the river and how Grandpa rode some twenty miles on horseback to find a doctor. "I swore I saw angels in the river that day," she said. "But the doctor said I must've dreamed them."

We had our noon meal right there under the lean-to with the kids, and I learned how Daddy's dark hair and blue eyes captured Mama the very first time they met. "I was sixteen," she said. "And here was this young man sitting on the ground in front of me, just smiling. The handsomest man I ever did see." She looked off toward the horizon, thoughtful-like. "Even then, something about him said he could do anything he set his mind to, legs or no legs." She laughed, and for a moment, she looked young as the girls at school. "Then he set his mind on me," she said, and laughed again.

By the time Daddy came in from the bay, Mama's cheeks had pinked up and her feet looked almost normal. He asked how she felt.

"Oh, for heaven's sake, John, I'm fine." She pointed to the fourteen jars cooling on the table. "And look at that. Our Sadie isn't a little girl anymore."

I locked the canner lid over the last seven jars and started supper. Mama and Daddy beamed their smiles at me. It felt like sunshine, and I soaked it up.

Chapter Twenty-Three

SHORTLY AFTER DADDY CAME home from fishing the next day, I saw him digging a hole into the side of the seawall.

"What's he doing, Mama?" I asked.

"We need a cool place to store all that duck we canned," she said. "We couldn't dig down deep enough for a root cellar without hitting tidewater, so Daddy got the bright idea to dig into the seawall." She laughed and her belly shook. "He's always surprising me."

I helped Mama carry our forty-two jars of duck to the new cellar, watched Daddy wedge scrap boards and tin into the opening to close it off, then start on another hole.

"For the Gillems," Mama said.

She looked like her old self again. The swelling in her ankles and feet had completely gone away.

Mrs. Gillem came carrying a box of jars across the lane, and Oren and Wyatt followed with more. I didn't see Dollie and figured she must be home looking after Caleb. While me and Jacob tramped back and forth, helping to fill the second cellar, I heard Mrs. Gillem ask Mama if she'd like to gather pecans with her at the river.

"The trees are thick along the Guadalupe," she said. "We could have pecan pie for Thanksgiving and sell the rest. Maybe make a little extra money for Christmas."

Mama nodded. "We'd better do it tomorrow, though, so the kids won't miss any more school."

"Are you sure you feel up to it that soon?" Mrs. Gillem asked.

Mama showed off her slender ankles. "I'm fine, now, but I'm not sure we could keep an eye on so many little ones around that river."

Mrs. Gillem agreed. "Rose Waller said she'd watch them for us, and we can give her a share of the pecans. It'll be fun," she said. "Just you and me, Dollie, and Sadie."

A nervous hope swelled inside me. This could be the chance I'd been waiting for. Only now, as I carried the Gillems' last three jars to their new root cellar, I worried that Dollie wouldn't want to be alone with me, that she'd ask to stay home.

Sunday morning, after Daddy and Jacob left for the bay, I gathered tow sacks and string for tying them off, a bucket and soap for washing up. Mama packed sandwiches, water, and two old quilts for resting under the trees. Her eyes shone bright, and her cheeks flushed rose-pink in the morning chill. She acted like gathering pecans was a picnic and not any kind of work at all. I would've felt the same way if I hadn't been fretting about how things would go with Dollie.

While I loaded the car, Mrs. Gillem came walking across the lane. She had a worried look on her face and I was sure she was going to tell us that Dollie wouldn't be going, but that wasn't it at all.

"Caleb's got a fever, Raine," she said. "I don't think it's bad, but I'd better stay home with him just in case it worsens. I can keep Emily and Bobby for you if you still want to go with the girls. No need to bother Rose with just your two."

Disappointment showed all over Mama's face, but she nodded and managed a smile. "Thank you, Irene. If the kids won't be too much trouble for you, we'll go."

"Good," Mrs. Gillem said. "Sadie, you round them up, and I'll take them with me right now."

I left her talking to Mama, telling her where the turnoff was to the river. I made sure the kids were clean and dressed and shooed them out the door.

Mrs. Gillem started home with Emily and Bobby in tow. "I'll send Dollie over soon as she lets Rose know we won't be needing her," she said. "And Sadie," she hollered over her shoulder, "you take good care of your mama, now."

"I will, Mrs. Gillem." I pulled in a deep breath and tried to quiet my worry. It was crazy for me to expect more of Dollie than I was willing to give Claudia, but I couldn't stop hoping. Before the day was over, I figured I'd know for sure whether there was a chance for Dollie and me.

When she came back from the Wallers', I took the backseat and let her sit up front with Mama. There wasn't much I didn't rattle on about during that ride. I kept thinking I could fill in the quiet spots and Mama wouldn't notice that things weren't quite right between me and Dollie. I couldn't tell whether she suspected the truth or not, but if she did, she didn't pry.

We drove past fenced pastures full of grazing cattle and furrowed fields of turnips and cabbages and onions. It seemed strange to me that rain could favor one place over another. Missouri had shriveled up like Mama's dried figs, but the fields here had been

< 207 >

blessed with enough rain to keep them green right into November.

By the time Mama found the turnoff to the river, two hours had passed. The sun had warmed the chill air, promising a good day for the work we'd be doing. She pulled off the pavement onto a dirt road that followed the river, and after driving a short way, she turned off the engine.

We sat in the quiet for a moment while black crows swooped from tree to tree, and chittering squirrels scrambled up branches dripping with Spanish moss. The still air smelled of river mud and waterlogged roots and moldering leaves. Doves cooed and blue-green dragonflies buzzed and darted. I heard an occasional ripple from the river, but I didn't hear a single seagull call. It surprised me to find I missed them.

Mama pushed open her door, and we ambled toward the sluggish river and back again. The few pecans we saw strewn about were hardly worth the gasoline it took to get us here. Mama pointed to tire tracks.

"Someone got here ahead of us," she said. "Let's try farther down."

We drove a good ways before we found a place that looked promising, and this time, Mama pulled up close to the trees.

The ground looked as if it had rained pecans. They popped and cracked beneath the tires as we rolled to a stop. We grabbed tow sacks and ran from the car, scooping up brown nuts. Mama headed off in one direction, and I followed Dollie down the other, thinking that finally we'd have a chance to talk. But Dollie left me behind, saying she'd go on down the river and work her way back.

I didn't argue. The day was early yet, and there'd be another chance. I made up my mind that when it came, I wouldn't let anything else stand in the way of my overdue apology. I pushed my thoughts toward pecan pies and the extra money we'd make, and slowly, my bag got heavier.

I don't know how much time passed before I thought to check on Mama. I tied off my first full sack of pecans, left it by the car, and took off down the opposite bank.

When I found a half-filled sack lying on the ground, I peered through the trees. "Mama?" I called, and listened.

A niggling worry squirmed inside me. I should've never left her alone. I jogged down the lower bank and hollered again, louder this time. "Mama, where are you?"

Birds fluttered away.

I doubled back, checking the higher bank where the ground was more level, and caught a glimpse of her yellow dress. I saw her sitting beneath a tree and relief breezed through me.

"Why didn't you answer me?" I called, running to her.

Her jaw tightened, her eyes scrunched up, and fear bolted through me. I hollered for Dollie and knelt at Mama's side. The pink in her cheeks I'd seen earlier had drained away.

"Oh, Mama," I whispered. "What is it?"

The tightness in her face eased. Dollie found us and squatted on the ground close by.

"It's the baby," Mama said, her voice still breathy.

"But it's too early—a whole month early," I said.

"Couldn't it be something else, Mrs. Wynn?" Dollie asked.

Mama shook her head. "The water around the baby broke."

Dollie sucked in a breath. "We've got to get you to Doc Roeder. I think I can drive us, Mrs. Wynn. Papa taught me."

Mama shook her head again. "It's too late."

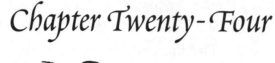

Chapter Twenty-Four

MAMA PULLED IN an uneven breath. "You girls will have to help me."

"But, Mama, I don't know what to do. I've never even seen a baby born."

Dollie's eyes stretched wide. "Me, either, Mrs. Wynn."

Mama's breath quickened again, and fear shot through me fast as lightning. Her pains were close. I knew that meant we didn't have much time. I glanced at Dollie and saw the terror I felt mirrored in her face.

Mama strained. "You've seen Ruby's puppies." Her brow wrinkled, and she squeezed her eyes closed. "Same . . . thing," she said through gritted teeth.

My mind flashed over the sticky-wet bundles that slid from Ruby's body, and I thought my heart would stop. Mama had already lost one baby. What if I did something wrong?

"I can't, Mama," I whispered. "I can't do it."

"You can." She pulled in a deep breath. "I'll be helping you." The lines in her face began to slide away. "Now listen close," she said, "before the next pain starts." She pulled herself up a bit. "Dollie?"

"Yes, ma'am?"

"Mr. Wynn always keeps matches in the car. Find them. We need a fire, downwind and away from us. Put enough of our drinking water in the wash bucket to boil the knife and a few feet of that string we brought to tie off the tow sacks. Quick now."

"Yes, ma'am." Dollie took off for the car.

"Sadie, dig a small hole right here beside me," she said. "The knife and cup will work well enough for that."

"A hole?" Panic sucked my breath away.

Mama's eyes softened. "Oh, Sadie. It's not for in case the baby dies. This is for cleaning up afterward, that's all."

Air filled my lungs again, but my legs wouldn't move.

"Hurry now," she said, tensing again.

I shrank from the pain in her face and ran for the car.

While Dollie started a fire and filled the bucket with some of our drinking water, I chiseled a hole in the hard clay next to Mama. When it was deep enough, she sent me to wash the knife and fetch the quilts.

Arms full, I ran back to her. "What now?" I asked. But another pain had already creased her face. She breathed hard like she was trying to blow out the hurt, and I waited, numb with fear.

"I'll need one quilt under me," she said finally, still panting. "Use the knife to rip up the other. We need scraps for cleaning up. And one big enough to wrap the baby in." She blew out a tired breath and her body slumped. "And give Dollie several rag-size pieces to boil. For cleaning the baby's nose and mouth."

I did as I was told, and all the while, I watched the pain come and go. Like a cat toying with a mouse, it would sink its teeth into her, hold her tight, and then let go, only to pounce on her all over again.

I remembered the way Ruby had labored for her pups. "Don't worry," Mama told me back then. "Her body knows exactly what to do." I ripped the quilt into scraps and prayed this would be true for Mama, too.

Soon the quilt pieces were ready. The knife, rags,

and string waited in the bucket of simmering water. In stops and starts, Mama hurried to tell us how to make sure the birth cord wasn't wrapped around the baby's neck. She panted through explanations of how to clean the nose and mouth before the shoulders came out. And with fingers trembling, she showed us how to tie a proper square knot, how to cut the cord, and how to make sure the baby was breathing.

I mopped Mama's brow and neck with a quilt scrap, and while I watched the pain strain her face and clench at her belly, sticky red puppies blurred my thoughts. My stomach knotted and my hands shook. How would I ever remember all she'd told me?

I looked up and caught Dollie watching me.

"Don't worry, Sadie," she whispered. "You're strong. Like your mama."

Hot tears rolled down my cheeks. Mama gripped my hand, and I brushed the wetness away before she could see how scared I was.

"It's . . . it's time," she whispered, squeezing the words between shallow breaths.

My heart pounded. I raced to the campfire with Dollie to wash up one last time and ran back to Mama with the bucket. I readied the clean quilt scraps beside me and knelt in front of Mama's open legs.

The baby's head crowned. I saw dark, wet hair.

"Oh, Mama, I can see it!"

She pulled in a breath, and her face turned red with strain.

The baby's head slipped out and turned sideways. Quickly, I slid a hand beneath the cheek and looked for a tangled cord.

Dollie handed me one of the sterile rags. "No cord, Mrs. Wynn," she reported.

I heard Mama panting while I cleaned out the mouth and wiped the little nose and eyes. Then she groaned, and the baby's upper shoulder came out. I slid my hand farther down the body to support it, and the other shoulder appeared. Before I could catch my breath the baby slid into my hands, and my heart leapfrogged into my throat.

Mama let out a long sigh. Her voice thready, she asked, "Is it breathing?"

I stared at the tiny blue thing still connected to Mama by the birth cord—the tiniest baby I'd ever seen. "I . . . I don't think so," I whispered.

"We need to rub it," Dollie said. "Hold the head down like your mama told us, and we'll get it to crying."

I held tight and lowered the slippery baby to a deep slant while Dollie rubbed the still, blue body, trying to coax air into its lungs. I hushed my own ragged breath and listened, but there was no sound.

Oh, please, God . . .

< 215 >

A rattle.

. . . please . . .

A gasp.

. . . help it breathe.

The little chest heaved, and my heart leaped.

Then came a mewing cry, and the tiny blue body flushed pink. Mama sighed again.

"Lay it down," Dollie said. "I'll cover it while you cut the cord."

I nodded, slid the crying baby onto Mama's belly, and with trembling fingers reached for the sterile string. I tied a square knot an inch from the baby's belly, tight like Mama told me. And another, three inches down the cord from that. I slid the knife between the two knots and cut the baby free. When I was sure there was no bleeding, I asked Mama if she was okay. She gave me a weary nod.

Dollie scooped the baby off Mama's belly and pulled the quilt piece around it. "It's a girl, Mrs. Wynn." Dollie turned to me and smiled. "Another sister."

I peered at the squirming, pink bundle, breathless at the doll-like fingers and toes, the tiny nose and mouth.

Mama pushed herself up a bit and held out her arms. "I think," she said, her voice still thin and wispy, "this little one has *two* big sisters now."

Dollie grinned so wide, I thought my heart would bust. She passed the baby to Mama, then handed her another sterile rag.

Mama cleaned and checked the tiny body head to toe. The crying stopped. When Mama was through, she bundled the baby up again. I saw worry flicker across her face then disappear, replaced by strain.

My stomach tightened all over again. "What is it, Mama?"

She shook her head. "Just the afterbirth."

"What do we do?"

Mama settled the baby close to her. "Leave the bucket and quilt scraps beside me and go wash up. I can take care of this while you load the car." She looked up at us and smiled around her discomfort. "Grace and I were blessed to have such strong young women with us."

Dollie grinned.

"Grace?" I asked.

Mama nodded and looked back at the squirming bundle by her side. "I think so," she said softly. "After your Grandmother Wynn." She flinched again and waved a hand at us. "Now go."

We washed up, grabbed Mama's half-filled bag of pecans, and ran down the river to gather up Dollie's. We tied the sacks off and together hefted them onto the floorboard—one in front, two in back. By the time we'd put out the fire, loaded everything we could, and got back to Mama, she was on her feet, leaning against the tree. The hole I'd dug was covered.

She pointed to the bucket and soiled quilt lying on the ground. "This is the last of it."

"I'll get it, Mrs. Wynn," Dollie said.

I picked up Grace, surprised all over again at how very small and light she felt. Dollie rolled up the quilt, stuffed it under her arm, and grabbed the bucket handle.

"Do you think you can drive that old car?" Mama asked her.

"Yes, ma'am. I believe I can."

"Good. Then we'd better get home. Sadie, you carry little Grace, and I'll lean on Dollie."

Dollie held out her free arm to Mama, and they started down the bank toward the car. Grace felt as delicate as Mama's rose-patterned teapot, and I followed slow and easy, already determined to do my best for her.

Every dozen steps or so, Mama would turn to check on us. She'd look at Grace, and I'd see that same bit of uneasiness in her eyes I'd seen before. It set me to worrying. I peered at the little face burrowed in the quilt scrap, wondering what Mama saw. Grace grabbed my finger with her own tiny ones, her grip strong. Except for being so little and the blue around her mouth, Grace looked fine to me.

When we finally reached the car, Dollie helped Mama ease across the backseat. She winced and settled her feet onto a sack of pecans.

"Can I get you some water before we leave, Mrs. Wynn?"

Mama shook her head. "I'll be fine till we get home, Dollie."

She held out her arms, and I handed Grace to her.

"We'd better get going," she said.

Dollie nodded and ran to start the car. I propped my feet on the sack of pecans on the front floorboard and watched Dollie stretch to reach the clutch. She shifted into first gear, and the car lurched forward. A soft "uh" sounded from the backseat.

"Dang," Dollie whispered under her breath.

She turned in a wide arc, pointed the car toward the dirt road, and shifted into second. The car lurched again, and Dollie cringed.

"I'll get the hang of it, Mrs. Wynn," she called over her shoulder. "Promise."

She gritted her teeth, and by the time we pulled onto the main road, she'd managed to even out the ride. She held the speed at thirty miles an hour, and at last I felt like I could breathe.

I glanced out the window. The sun still sat rather

high in the sky. Two o'clock, I guessed, maybe three. Daddy and Jacob probably weren't home from fishing yet. I smiled. They'd be so surprised!

I looked over my shoulder at Mama. She had Grace hugged up, watching her closely, but I couldn't ignore the worried look in her eyes any longer. I had to know. "What is it, Mama?" I asked. "What's wrong?"

Mama studied Grace. "I'm sure she's fine, Sadie."

She smiled at me, but the smile never reached her eyes.

"Wouldn't hurt to let Dr. Roeder look at her before we go home, though," she said.

"It's Sunday, Mrs. Wynn," Dollie said. "But he's probably home. We'll check and see."

"Thank you, Dollie. That'll be fine."

A sickening flutter hit my belly. I turned back around, sure now that nothing at all was fine.

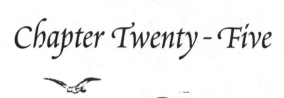

Chapter Twenty - Five

WORRY PULLED AT ME all the way to Dr. Roeder's house. He answered the door and peered at Grace through his thick glasses.

"Myrt," he called down the hall, "I'll be needing your help."

He steered Mama into a room off the entry and left me and Dollie in the parlor. Mrs. Roeder, wiping her hands on her apron, bustled after them. Before she disappeared through the door, I glimpsed glass-fronted cabinets filled with bottles and an examining table draped in white sheets.

The whole house smelled of rubbing alcohol. But underneath that I caught the clean scent of furniture polish and floor wax. Ruffled curtains billowed lightly at the windows, and wood floors, shiny bright, reflected the evening light. I sat next to Dollie on the edge of a carved cherry-wood love seat covered in gold brocade. I folded my hands in my lap and waited.

After a short while Mrs. Roeder hurried out again.

"Oh, my," she said. "My, my." She leaned through the parlor doorway. "Well, come on now. Come with me." She waved us to our feet and down the hall. "What a day you two have had!"

Dollie gave me a dazed look. I shrugged, and hurried into the kitchen after Mrs. Roeder.

"Sit down, sit down." She waved a hand at the table, pulled ham and milk from the icebox and a loaf of light bread from the cabinet. "Delivering babies is hard work, even for Dr. Roeder." She buttered bread and layered on thick slices of ham. "You must be starving by now."

Dollie grinned behind Mrs. Roeder's back. "Um . . . well, yes, ma'am," she said. "I guess it *has* been a while since we've eaten."

Mrs. Roeder set the sandwiches on the table and went back for tall glasses of cold milk. "Now you finish that off, and I'll get you a nice slice of chocolate cake. Made it just this morning." She turned, eyes wide with surprise. "About the time you two were bringing that sweet little sister of yours into the world, I'll bet." She laughed, placed another sandwich and more milk on a tray, and hurried off.

Dollie glanced at me, her smile gone. "You don't suppose she *really* thinks we're sisters, do you? Us being so different and all?"

I watched her take a big bite out of her sandwich. "I wish we were," I whispered under my breath. I glanced to see if she'd heard me, but she kept on eating.

By the time we'd finished our chocolate cake, Dr. Roeder walked into the kitchen, wiping his forehead with a white handkerchief. I held my breath.

"Well, your mother tells me you two did a fine job." He stuffed the hankie into his back pocket and smiled. "Don't think I could've done much better myself."

I breathed again. "Will the baby be all right?" I asked.

He peered at me over the rim of his glasses. "We'll get to that. But first, I need to talk about you and how you can help. Your mama needs to spend her time looking after herself and that baby. That means she needs someone to do the cooking and cleaning for a while. Think you can handle that?"

I nodded. "Yessir. But the baby. Is she okay?" I asked again.

"You just do what your mama tells you. That's the best way to help little Grace."

I frowned, and opened my mouth to complain, but he shooed us back to the parlor where Mama waited. On a side table sat the tray Mrs. Roeder had hurried off with, hardly touched.

"Now, which of you girls did the driving?" the doctor asked.

"I did, Dr. Roeder," Dollie said.

"Do you think you can make it home the rest of the way?"

She nodded. "Yessir. I can do it."

"Good. Then let's get you loaded up."

He helped Mama down the steps and into the car, then stepped aside so Mrs. Roeder could pass the baby through. Dollie started the car, and I scrambled into the front seat.

Leaning against the open door, Dr. Roeder bent to look in at Mama. "Mind what I say now, Mrs. Wynn. Don't you get too attached now."

I glared at him, finally understanding what it was he wouldn't tell me in the kitchen. He didn't think Grace would live.

Mama understood, too, and her pale face showed it. She cuddled Grace, and without even a word or a glance at Dr. Roeder, she jerked the door from under his hand and slammed it shut. Dollie pulled out onto the road and left him standing with Mrs. Roeder by their white picket fence.

Mama's face told me all I needed to know. She'd never give up on Grace, no matter what that stupid doctor thought. None of us would. And especially not me.

By the time we'd pulled onto our lane, evening shadows had stretched to the seawall. Daddy sat under the lean-to, working on a shrimp net, his face golden in the dying light. When he saw Dollie pull up to the house, he flung the net aside, lowered his head, and swung his body toward the car.

Face grim, he waited, his eyes fixed on Mama. She passed Grace to Dollie, eased herself across the seat, and stood, smiling at Daddy. I saw him pull in a sharp breath, like he'd felt death flutter past.

She pointed to the bundle. "We have a new baby girl, John."

"It's too soon," he said. "Is she all right?"

Mama's eyes glinted with determination. "She will be," she said. "Where are the kids?"

"At the Gillems', eating supper."

Mama nodded. "Let's get inside so you can see her." She stepped through the doorway and eased herself into the rocking chair.

Dollie followed, put Grace in Mama's arms, and gave her a hug. "She's wonderful, Mrs. Wynn."

Mama squeezed Dollie's hand. "So are you," she whispered.

Dollie grinned and turned to leave.

While Mama showed the baby to Daddy, I sat on the bench outside and watched Dollie walk across the lane. This morning nothing had been more important than the two of us.

Now nothing mattered but Grace.

Mrs. Gillem offered to keep the kids awhile. After they all had a peek at the baby and Jacob had fetched fresh water, they left to sleep on pallets at the Gillems' house. It was a big help, but our little house seemed empty without them.

The lamp burned low all night. Mama stayed in bed, but I knew she wasn't resting. She was awake when I climbed into the loft, nursing when I got up later to go to the outhouse, and awake again when I started Daddy's breakfast. She lay there, watching Grace breathe in and out.

I understood from the first that I'd have to stay home from school. Mama fretted over it till Dollie said she'd bring home a list of our assignments and return my work every morning.

I cooked and cleaned, washed diapers, and did the mending. And when supper dishes were done, I did my schoolwork. I took to caring for the baby, too, between feedings so Mama would rest. But before she'd even close her eyes, I had to promise to watch Grace every minute. Dr. Roeder had told Mama the blue color was a sign of breathing problems. He said lots of premature babies died in their sleep. But Mama was determined that this wouldn't happen to our Grace. She said we were gonna prove that doctor wrong.

So while Mama napped, I rocked Grace and sang to her. Her baby fingers curled around mine, and her blue eyes studied me like she was storing up the words to every song. But mostly she slept, and I watched her little chest rise and fall.

I hadn't given Thanksgiving a single thought till Wednesday, when Mrs. Gillem made her usual evening visit to see how we were getting on.

She glanced around the house, smiling with approval, then turned to Mama. "Sadie's still taking good care of you, I see," she said. "But I don't want you worrying about tomorrow. I've been baking pecan pies today, and come daybreak, Dan's going to get us some fresh duck to stuff. We'll have our dinner right here under your lean-to like we planned." She bent down to look at Grace. "How's this little one doing?"

Mama pulled the blanket back, and Mrs. Gillem looked closely. "Don't you worry, Raine," she whispered, patting Mama's arm. "She'll do just fine."

Mama nodded, but we'd both seen the troubled look on Mrs. Gillem's face.

She straightened up and headed for the door. "I'll send Dollie and Davis over to help set up the tables tomorrow. But in the meantime, Sadie, you just keep helping your mama like you've been doing."

"Yes, ma'am."

"And holler if you need me."

"Thanks, Mrs. Gillem."

I walked her out, raised an arm to wave at Bobby and Tanner playing across the lane, and felt my hand tremble.

It was easy to see that Mrs. Gillem, a woman who had birthed seven children, was worried about our Grace, worried about her breathing and the blue color around her mouth and fingernails.

What if Dr. Roeder was right? What if nothing we did was enough and Grace slipped away from us in her sleep?

I sat outside, where Mama couldn't see me, and I cried.

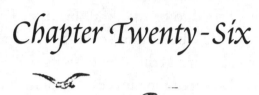

Chapter Twenty-Six

GRACE'S FOURTH NIGHT in this world passed with hardly a sound. I thought it was a good sign till I heard Mama pacing the floor with her, whispering, coaxing her to breathe. I finally got up, too, and since I could do nothing else, I made coffee for Daddy. He watched from bed, eyes clouded and jaw tight with worry.

The dark morning slipped away, and finally the troubled lines on Mama's face did, too. Grace's little chest rose and fell, steady as the tick of a clock. The blue color warmed to pink, and she nursed. When she was done, Mama breathed a tired sigh and put her in my arms. I rocked her and watched her sleep till the sun peeked through the windows.

We took turns tending the baby that long morning while across the lane Mr. Gillem and Davis sat on upturned buckets in the cool, dry air, cleaning fresh ducks and shucking oysters for our Thanksgiving dinner. I tried to be thankful this day of all days, but with Grace's breathing so fluttery, all this fuss about a meal seemed trifling and foolish.

Even so, I savored the hints of pumpkin and cinnamon drifting across to us from Mrs. Gillem's oven. And I didn't mind seeing Davis arrange our two long tables end to end. Or watching Dollie drape them with her mama's embroidered tablecloths.

Mama watched, too, and after a while, her spirits lifted. She smiled. At me, at Grace, at Daddy, at Davis when he brought over Caleb's high chair, and even at the seagulls pestering Mr. Gillem while he worked. I looked at our new baby, asleep in my arms, her wispy dark lashes fringed against pink cheeks, and I had to smile, too. Seems I was thankful, after all. For the bloom in her baby face. For the easy rhythm in her tiny chest. And even for the dinner the Gillems were working so hard to prepare.

Mama let me brush and braid her shiny hair and pin it around the back of her head like a halo. Then I put on my morning-glory dress and helped bundle Grace into her basket.

Soon, dressed in our best, we all found our places

around the loaded table. Seven-month-old Caleb sat in his high chair, banging a spoon against the wooden tray, and Grace lay between Mama and Daddy, sleeping through the noise.

A platterful of roasted ducks stuffed with oyster dressing sat in the middle of the table. And around it, I saw steaming biscuits and greens, sweet potatoes and corn, and ruby-red cranberry sauce. Behind us, on Mr. Winslow's rickety table, pumpkin and pecan pies waited, draped with cup towels.

Mrs. Gillem, her face still rosy from all the cooking, waited till everyone was seated to join us.

"I never saw such a fine-looking dinner, Irene," Mama said. "You come sit down, now, and enjoy it with us."

She nodded. "I'm coming. Just wanted to take a last look at the pretty picture we make gathered around this table." Satisfied, she finally squeezed in beside Mr. Gillem.

Dollie and Davis sat opposite me, side by side. I hadn't been this close to Davis since that day on the playground, and seeing him brought back the shameful way I'd treated Dollie. I stole glances at him when he joked with Jacob. I smiled at the gentle-hearted teasing he gave Wyatt and the way he laughed out loud at one of Daddy's stories, but I never once saw him look at me. I didn't blame him. I didn't care to look at Claudia again, either, after all she'd done. How could I expect any more from him?

But still, I wanted it.

Mr. Gillem reached for hands on either side of him, and we all did the same. It got so quiet around the table you could hear music from Ma Beasley's jukebox down on the harbor road.

"Today," Mr. Gillem said, his voice deep and solemn, "we come to this table thankful." Caleb banged his spoon against his tray again and grinned at his papa.

"In these hard times, when so many go homeless and hungry, our families have been blessed." He looked at each one of us kids. "Let your prayers today be for those hungry souls. And for little Grace." His voice turned thick and tight. "May the good Lord make her strong and healthy."

"Amen," Daddy whispered, and a whole chorus of amens echoed after him.

Mr. Gillem, his eyes full and glistening, smiled at Mama and Daddy. Then, blinking away the wet shine, he clapped his hands together. "Now we're gonna eat like kings!" He held his thin belly and laughed like jolly King Cole. Then he called to "Prince Bobby" and "Duke Tanner" to pass their plates while he halved roasted ducks and spooned out stuffing.

I filled my plate, but I couldn't help thinking of

Wilma and Mr. Sparrow. I hoped they sat at a table as full as this one, but mostly, I hoped they were with folks as good as these.

We ate till the table was a mess of bones and empty dishes, then we held our bellies and groaned at our greediness, too full to give Mrs. Gillem's pies the appreciation they deserved. We decided they'd make a right nice supper, however, and left them sitting on Mr. Winslow's old table to tempt us as the day wore on.

We cleaned up quick with all the kids helping, and after we'd rested a bit, Daddy sent Jacob for the fiddle. I went in to check on Mama and found her rocking Grace. Her eyelids drooped and her head nodded, reminding me of how little sleep she'd had.

I reached for the baby. "Let me have her, Mama. You go rest awhile."

With a grateful smile, she slipped Grace into my arms. "Watch her close now," she said, like she always did.

I nodded and answered like always. "I will, Mama."

Dollie knocked lightly and stuck her head in the open doorway. "I'd be happy to help out awhile, Mrs. Wynn," she said.

Stifling a yawn, Mama crawled onto her bed. "That'd be nice, Dollie; thank you. I'll just leave you two to work it out." She closed her eyes and rolled over.

Dollie glanced at me. "Want me to spell you a bit?" she whispered.

I opened my mouth, but when nothing came out, I nodded instead. I eased the baby into Dollie's arms and moved aside so she could sit in the rocking chair.

"Is there anything special I need to do?"

"Just watch real close. Make sure she's breathing smooth and regular."

Dollie nodded, settled back, and peeked around the blanket at Grace.

I glanced at Mama, already sleeping soundly. Maybe the time had finally come for me and Dollie to talk. My heart skittered as I sat on the floor across from her, and words tumbled wild in my head.

Daddy finished his tuning and started right up with "Baby Face." It was for Mama and Grace, I was sure, but they slept right through it.

While Dollie rocked and Daddy played, I struggled to get my thoughts straight and find the courage to say what I'd been wanting to for weeks. Then between songs when the house was quiet, Dollie looked up from Grace's tiny face and said, "She looks like you."

My newly planned words flew right out of my head. I sat there blinking, feeling foolish. "I thought she looked like Daddy," I said finally.

"Well, sure she does. You do, too, with your dark hair and blue eyes." She studied Grace again. "Ain't hard to see she'll be another beauty."

Outside, someone asked Daddy to play "Sweet Georgia Brown" and the fiddling started up again.

Dollie ran a finger over Grace's tiny hand. "Papa said we shouldn't worry. He says God never sends a trial without a blessing." She sighed and looked up at me. "I've thought about that a lot since that day on the playground."

I looked away, ashamed, though she'd said it without a flicker of blame.

"I reckon," she went on, "my helping to bring a baby into the world should be blessing enough for losing a friend."

I hung my head, and tears dripped onto my dress. Morning glories turned wet and dark. "I wish I could take it all back," I whispered.

Dollie stiffened, then sat straight up. Confused, I did, too.

"Something's wrong," she said.

She stared at Grace, her eyes wide and unblinking, and I leaped to my feet.

"She's not breathing, Sadie. She's not breathing!"

I pitched my voice above Daddy's fiddle and yelled for Mama. She jerked upright. "It's Grace, Mama! Hurry!"

In seconds she had bounded to her feet and pulled the limp blue body from Dollie's arms. "Get your daddy," she said to me.

I stumbled through the door and around the empty tables, yelling for Daddy. His bow squawked to a stop and dangled above the strings. "Grace isn't breathing!" I shouted, and in the silent seconds that followed, the dreadful words pounded in my ears.

Dollie shoved benches aside. "This way, Mr. Wynn."

He dropped the fiddle and swept himself to the ground and into the house. Mr. and Mrs. Gillem hurried after him.

Jacob stood beside Davis and Oren, a stricken look on his face, and Emily buried her frightened tears in Dollie's dress. I tried to pray, but words fluttered in my head like startled gulls.

I glanced at Dollie and Davis. Then back at the house. Dollie was wrong. This trial had no blessing. Grace stopped breathing in her sleep, just like the doctor warned. And now she was dead.

A wretched anguish welled up and choked the air out of me. I turned and ran up the seawall trail. I thrashed through the cedars. Greedy branches ripped at morning glories, ripped at skin, and held me fast till all I could do was drop to my knees.

Chapter Twenty-Seven

"Sadie?"

Dollie's voice.

"Sadie, are you up here?"

Davis, too.

"Please answer, Sadie."

Dollie again. Go away.

"We need to talk to you."

I don't want to hear. I squeezed my eyes shut. *I don't want to know.*

"The baby's breathing fine now."

I turned toward the sound, unsure of what I'd heard. Caked blood cracked. Scratches stung.

"Sadie, please come out."

Davis's voice vibrated through me. Cedars rustled.

"Here," he said, reaching for me.

Hands lifted.

Dollie held back hungry branches. "This way," she said and helped Davis lead me to the road's edge.

I sat, and my knee rested on crushed oyster shell like it did on Halloween. I looked for the orange moon and saw only a twilight sky.

"Did you hear?" he asked.

I stared at him.

"Grace is fine now."

"She . . . she didn't die?" my voice croaked, dry and raspy.

Dollie smiled and shook her head. "That baby's the healthiest pink you ever did see. She's busy making up for missing her Thanksgiving dinner, but your mama's been worried about you."

I sucked in a breath. Grace was alive. She was home in Mama's arms.

"Doc doesn't know why she quit breathing," Davis said. "He reckons some babies just can't bear leaving heaven to get born."

"But he checked her over real careful," Dollie added. "Even after everything that happened today, he said her little lungs seemed to be working better now."

I closed my eyes, thankful, but beneath the relief, guilt still plagued me. "I think it might've been my fault," I whispered.

Dollie frowned. "What do you mean? Your mama told everyone how careful you tended her. Even the doc said it was your fast call for help that saved her."

I shook my head, and my swollen eyes welled up again. "I said those awful things to you on the playground. I acted as mean as Claudia." Sobs jerked at my chest. "I sowed misery, and we almost lost Grace."

Dollie and Davis didn't say a word while I cried. Then, in the awful quiet that followed, I heard Davis growl. "Aw, Sadie."

My head snapped up.

He stood over me, scowling. "That's the battiest thing I ever heard. You might've sowed some misery all right, but not near as much as you heaped on yourself. And nothing you did made Grace sick." He shook a finger in my face. "Nothing."

I flinched and watched him pace across the shell road. He blew out an impatient breath, looked out over the harbor, and shook his head. Then, peering at me from the corner of his eye, he huffed and tossed me a crooked grin. "It made *me* pretty sick, though."

Dollie laughed. "Me too. But I heard you say you wished you could take it all back."

My head bobbed. "I did . . . I do . . . but I didn't think—"

"Now you're getting it," Davis said, back in my face. "You sure enough didn't think." His eyes flashed, but his gaze quickly softened and fell to his feet. "I guess none of us did."

Dollie sighed. "We knew something had to be wrong, Sadie. You had to be plumb miserable to have said the things you did. It wasn't like you at all."

It wasn't like me? I blinked, confused.

"If we'd just talked it out, we could've put all this foolishness to rest." Dollie gave me a wistful look. "I should've tried to do that for you, Sadie. I should've helped you with whatever was troubling you. I'm sorry." She looked at Davis. "We're both sorry."

Davis nodded.

"*You're* sorry?" I shook my head. "But I'm the one—"

"Aw, for crying out loud, Sadie. We all made mistakes. How long are we gonna drag this out?" He gave me a hard look. "Are we friends or not?"

I stared at him, then glanced at Dollie, uncertain. "You're really not mad?"

Dollie shrugged. "Never was, really. You were mad enough for all three of us."

I cringed, and Dollie laughed.

"Besides," Davis said, "you told the best ghost story I ever heard. For a girl, that is."

"Hey, you'd better watch that 'for a girl' stuff." Dollie stood and brushed off her dress. "Grace is going to need you to set an example, help her learn she's as good as anybody in this town. Even you."

"Okay, okay," Davis muttered. "No one's gonna say I didn't do my part."

While they teased and joked, I tried to take in all they'd just said.

Grace was okay. I breathed in the wonder of that, happier than I could ever remember.

But there was more. Dollie and Davis still wanted me as a friend, too. The idea that they'd been worried about me all that time left me totally bewildered. How could they see past my shameful behavior to what was truly in my heart?

I guess Mama had been proven right again. Who you are inside does show through. Seems Dollie and Davis saw a shine in me I never knew was there, and they trusted that. The whole thing made my head spin just thinking of it.

I'd learned a lot from them about myself, and about friendship and forgiveness, too. But I could see now that there was a whole lot more to learn.

Davis held out a hand. "Time to go home," he said.

I slipped my hand in his and let him pull me up. We started down the seawall trail together, and the smell of clean green water followed on the breeze. Just ahead, I heard whispers and giggles, counting and scurrying feet.

". . . eight, nine, ten. Here I come!" Ethan shouted. "Ready or not!"

Lamplight glowed from the windows in our little house—from windows all down our lane—and I finally understood what I'd been feeling in my heart for weeks.

I didn't want to be anyplace else.

Chapter Twenty-Eight

I STAYED HOME another week to help watch over Grace, but by the beginning of December, Mama put her foot down and sent me off to school. Two-week-old Grace hadn't had another bad spell, and though we still watched her close, we'd begun to feel more confident about her wanting to stay in this world.

My first day back in class was strange. Mrs. Doogan hugged me and whispered how glad she was to have me back. Kids who had never bothered to speak to me before smiled or waved from across the room. And Gunther called me "Dr. Wynn." I glanced at Dollie, full of questions, but she just grinned.

Later, by the steps to the playground, Lucy Peardon grabbed me. "Dollie told us all about your baby sister, Sadie. How you had to deliver the tiny thing all by yourself on that riverbank." She put a hand on her chest. "I never would've been so brave."

I shrugged. "We didn't have much choice, really."

While Lucy talked to Dollie, I saw Claudia sitting on the steps with her friends, a sour look on her face. I knew she'd been listening to us, but she tried not to let on. Claudia was, after all, Claudia.

I found myself wondering what made her so ornery. True, I'd done some foolhardy things myself 'cause I lost my home and my best friend. Maybe something like that haunted Claudia, too. Whatever her ghosts were, I felt sure she'd hang on to her bitterness, same as me, till a trial big enough showed her how foolish she was being. I felt sorry for her. She couldn't possibly have friends as good as Dollie and Davis to help her figure it all out.

Confusion squirmed inside me. Was I really feeling sorry for Claudia? Surprise must've shown all over me, 'cause she tossed me a real strange look. But when I thought about it, I understood the reason for my sympathy. Claudia and I shared a common misery. We'd both carried the weight of mean words around with us, and I knew all too well the torment that caused.

Wouldn't she be dumbfounded to know how alike we'd been all this time? I grinned at her just thinking of it, and then it was her turn to look confused.

At home, Mama took over the simple chores, the ones that let her keep Grace close by, and Dollie helped me with the rest when I got home from school.

The next few weeks disappeared in a blur of cooking and cleaning up, laundry and studying for tests I'd missed, and best of all, listening to Dollie's stories while I rocked Grace.

I finally told Dollie about Wilma, about how I'd waited for letters that never came, and how I'd tried to keep my promise to always be her best friend.

"It was foolish of me and hurtful to you," I said, "but that promise was all I had left of her. Now I don't even have that."

The rocker creaked under me while Dollie nodded, slow and thoughtful. "It's not easy finding a safe place to put a promise that big. I know. I lost friends, too, Annie and Claire Marie, when their families struck out from Ohio looking for work."

I flinched, ashamed that I hadn't considered the friends she'd been forced to give up.

"But Papa said they weren't really lost at all, that they'd be with me for as long as I wanted them." She sat on the floor in front of me, cross-legged. "They're with us even now. And Wilma is, too."

I blinked, confused, and she smiled at my puzzlement.

"I'll share Annie and Claire Marie with you," she

explained, "and you can share Wilma with me." She shrugged. "That way we can all be best friends."

I stopped rocking and felt my weighty promise shift inside me. Prickles crawled up my neck, and I shivered like a wind from heaven had blown over me. Simple as her answer was, I knew the good Lord must've had a hand in it. Only He would've thought of choosing Dollie to help me keep my promise.

"Now," Dollie said, her green eyes full, "tell me all about Wilma."

Chapter Twenty-Nine

COOL NORTHERS KEPT the heat away, and soon store owners painted their windows with red poinsettias, reindeer, and rosy-cheeked Santas. Behind the glass, clerks set up dolls dressed in fur-trimmed coats and toy trains that chugged through tunnels and past stations sprinkled with fake snow.

When I was alone in the house, I took my mason jar off the shelf and counted my money. After weeks of trying to decide how to spend it, I'd finally come up with a perfect idea. Later, I asked Mama if I could come home late on Wednesday evening.

She eyed my empty jar and smiled. "I guess that would be okay. Are you doing some Christmas shopping?"

I kept my mouth shut and just nodded, afraid if I got started, I'd give away my secret for sure.

On Wednesday afternoon, December 21, the last school day before Christmas vacation, Mrs. Doogan let us sit anywhere we liked. Claudia jumped up and was gone in a flash to join her friends, so Dollie grabbed the empty seat behind me. Mrs. Doogan passed out lemonade and sugar cookies shaped like stars. We nibbled our treats, relishing every bite, and talked about the Christmas ornaments and chain garlands we'd make out of red and green construction paper for our own trees.

When the bell rang, I had to tell Dollie I wouldn't be walking home with her and the kids.

"Secrets?" she asked.

I shrugged. "It's Christmas."

"Don't worry," she said. "I'll cover for you."

When they were gone, I walked to the lumberyard and talked to Mr. Fields. He looked surprised when I told him what I wanted, but he helped me figure up everything I'd need. He even said he'd be happy to deliver it himself on Christmas Eve, since they'd be closing a bit early that day.

"I don't think I ever heard tell of a kid planning a gift like this before," he said. "I'm gonna enjoy seeing the surprised look on your mama's and daddy's faces."

After I paid for my order, I had forty-six cents left. It was enough to get a little something for each of the kids and the Gillems, too, so I walked to Warren's Five and Dime before heading home.

A bell jingled when I opened the door, and a young woman looked up from behind a glass case. "Can I help you find something?"

I nodded. "Yes, please."

I walked past fabric and leather belts to the glass case that held jars of stick candy and jawbreakers, boxes of caramels and chocolates. "I'd like to pick out something sweet for my brothers and sisters."

After much deliberation, I chose a big nickel chocolate bar for each of the kids' stockings, a big box of striped ribbon candy for the Gillems, and a pink bow for Grace's dark hair.

The lady wrapped the ribbon candy in brown paper for me and tied it off with a twine bow. "White paper snowflakes would dress up that brown paper real nice," she said.

Pleased with the idea, I said, "Thank you, ma'am. I'll do just that."

When I got home, Mama and Daddy and all the kids were sitting outside under the lean-to. Daddy cradled five-week-old Grace in his arms, and I swear, every face I looked at was grinning, even Grace's.

"We just got back from Dr. Roeder's," Mama said. "He listened to Grace's lungs and said she was healthy as any baby he'd ever seen."

"Oh, Mama," I whispered. I dropped my bag at my feet and wrapped my arms around her. "It's the best Christmas present ever."

She squeezed me tight, and Bobby and Emily jumped up and down, yelling "Hooray!" so loud Grace cried. We ran to Daddy, laughing at Grace's howls and scarlet face.

"Look at that," Daddy said, holding her up. "No more blue for this girl. It's Christmas red from now on."

We laughed again, and Mama's face opened full as the blooms on Mr. Caughlin's hibiscus bush.

That weekend Daddy cut a small cedar from the seawall and nailed it to a wooden stand he'd made. The cedar didn't quite measure up to the pines we had back home, but you could hardly tell the difference once we added paper ornaments and draped it with our red-and-green chains. Mama set the tree on our wobbly table, up against the wall, joking all the while about how Bobby and Emily would have to eat their meals under cedar branches, like rabbits, till Christmas was over. After that remark, of course, they hopped everywhere, noses twitching, nibbling at imaginary carrots.

I woke up early the next day, too excited about Mr. Fields' delivery to sleep. I crept from bed in my bare feet, turned the lamp low, and mixed up pancakes for breakfast in the dim light. I covered the batter with a cup towel and went outside to wait for Daddy to wake up. Warm, damp air lapped at me, making a white Christmas seem like a faraway dream. But yesterday evening, Mr. Hauke's radio had said the weather would turn cool again tonight, just in time for our party.

Down the lane, I saw lamplight brighten the Wallers' window. Daddy would be up soon, too. Mama had wanted him to stay home today, but he'd said no.

"One more fishing day," he told her, "and we'll have enough to pay Mr. Fields the rest of what we owe him."

"But it's Christmas Eve, John."

"Don't worry, Raine. I haven't forgotten." He grinned and patted her on the knee. "Me and Jacob will be home early, and we'll have our party."

Mama sighed.

I think she loved Christmas Eve even better than Christmas Day. She loved the storytelling and the carols. And she always sat on quilts with the little ones, watching through the window for Santa's sleigh till eyes turned too sleepy and full of dreams to stay

< 251 >

awake. I loved it, too, those magic hours before Christmas morning. Especially this year, 'cause Dollie and Davis would be here sharing it with me.

But right then, while most everyone still slept, it was the lumberyard's four o'clock closing I was dreaming of. When Mr. Fields would lock his doors, get in his truck, and come rumbling onto our lane with my surprise.

The steamy morning inched into afternoon, and Daddy still wasn't home. By three o'clock, I was sure God had never made a longer, more worrisome day. But when four o'clock finally arrived, I lost all hope. I slumped onto the bench outside, cutting out paper snowflakes to glue on the Gillems' package.

Then I heard someone shout, "Ho, ho, ho!"

My head jerked up. Daddy and Jacob were coming down the seawall trail.

"Merry Christmas," Daddy called.

"Got us some oysters for supper, Mama," Jacob hollered, holding up a quart jar. He often shucked oysters while Daddy fished.

They came down the trail, wearing big grins. I guess by then I wore one of my own.

Daddy winked at Mama and patted his pocket. "Got the last of Mr. Fields' money right here," he said, "and a bit extra to boot."

I thought Mama would fuss about his working so late on Christmas Eve, but I guess she was too relieved to have him home. I was, too. She gave him a hug, and while he washed up, she poured him a cup of coffee.

Keeping a close watch on the road, I ladled water into a bowl and began washing the grit out of the oysters. I'd hardly got started before I heard a rumble. I whirled around, slinging water in Jacob's face.

"Hey!" He wiped the splatter on his shirtsleeve. "Watch what you're doing, will ya?"

"Sorry." I brushed past him and peered at the truck coming down the road. It was Mr. Fields, all right. He turned onto our lane, and Daddy raised a curious eye, watching over the rim of his coffee cup. When Mr. Fields stopped in front of our lean-to and got out, all the kids came running to see what was being delivered.

Daddy sat by the storage box, and Mama stood beside him, confused looks on both of their faces.

"Merry Christmas!" Mr. Fields boomed. He nodded at Mama and Daddy. "Got a delivery here for Mr. and Mrs. Wynn."

Daddy's face puzzled up. He shook his head. "That can't be for me, Ben."

Mr. Fields bent to look at his invoice, but not before I caught the twinkle in his eyes.

"Well, that's strange, John, 'cause this here piece of paper has your name on it. Bought and paid for three days ago. To be delivered December twenty-fourth. That's today, ain't it?" Mr. Fields pressed his lips together, trying not to smile.

Daddy looked plumb dumbfounded. "What is it?"

"Well, I guess you'll have to ask the young lady who paid for it."

My heart pounded, and Mr. Fields grinned so big, all I could see was teeth.

"I think your daddy has some questions for you, Sadie."

Daddy gave me an astonished look. "You bought lumber?"

I nodded. "Mr. Fields helped me pick out the boards."

"Got some mighty nice pine here, John," Mr. Fields said. "Clear and fine as any I've sold." He pulled the boards from the back of the truck.

"What for?" Daddy asked me.

I glanced at Mama, my stomach all aflutter, then back at Daddy. "For Mama's table. For our new life."

Daddy stared at me a moment, his eyes shiny. He held out his arms, and I slipped into their strong circle. Then Mama had her arms around me, too. She kissed me and left my cheek wet with her tears.

"Merry Christmas," I whispered.

I felt Daddy's arms tighten. "Merry Christmas, Babygirl."

Chapter Thirty

EVERYTHING WAS READY. I'd finished gluing my snow-flakes on the package of ribbon candy and put it under our tree for the Gillems. I'd give it to them after the party, before they went home. The chocolate bars and Grace's pink bow lay hidden in the storage box, waiting for tonight. While everyone slept, I'd sneak my gifts into the Christmas stockings we'd hung from the loft.

Inside, Grace lay snuggled in her basket beside Mama and Daddy, sleeping while they made plans for the new table. And outside, Jacob hunched over a game of marbles with Oren and Wyatt, waiting for the party to begin. I guess we were all feeling a bit antsy. I even saw Davis throwing a ball against the outhouse door, sending his anxious *thump, thump, thump* echoing down the lane.

Everything was perfect. Or at least it appeared so.

I decided to take the trail up the seawall to watch for the coming norther. I loved the way the bay slicked off and light played across its glassy surface just before the north wind hit. But the real magic happened when the first cool gust swept across the water, breathing life into it, making it dance again.

When I reached the top of the seawall, I saw gulls and blue herons resting on dock pilings along the harbor's edge, looking as if they didn't have a single worry in their heads. I felt a gnawing envy. Most everyone I knew had at least one worry they couldn't get shed of. Mine was not knowing what happened to Wilma.

But then there was Mr. Sparrow, too.

I glanced down the maintenance road to where his box had once been. Almost four months had passed since I'd seen him last. I knew it was crazy to fret over something I couldn't change, but this man had lost a home and loved ones, just like me. And I knew what that felt like.

I never had a meal that I didn't wonder if he was hungry, too. And every time I looked at our cardboard walls, I remembered that day on the seawall and my surprise at finding a grown man sleeping in a box.

I inched closer to the place I'd first seen him so long ago, and a bright reflection winked beneath the cedars. I shielded my eyes against the fading sun and squinted. A bottle cap? Or an old can, maybe? I moved branches aside for a closer look, and my heart leaped.

It was Mr. Sparrow's tin.

I spun around, searching, hoping I could catch just one glimpse of him before he disappeared again. I ran down the maintenance road and peered up and down the harbor below.

But he was nowhere.

I walked back, my head full of *why*s and *when*s and *maybe*s. Maybe the box had been here all along, and I just never noticed. He could've left it behind months ago, empty. Or maybe it wasn't even the same one.

Down below the seawall, I heard happy shouts. Daddy's fiddle tuning had begun. The party had started without me, and I needed to hurry.

I kneeled and reached through the cedars, my fingers fumbling and clumsy. I clutched the rusty tin, pulled it out, and my hopes sank.

It felt light.

It felt empty.

I raised the box to my ear, tilted it to one side, and listened. Something slid across the bottom. While Santa's merry eyes watched, I tucked the tin between my knees and gripped the edge. With a quick tug, the lid slid aside.

I stared at a torn piece of notebook paper lying on top, and for a moment, I couldn't breathe. Without touching it, I read:

> FRIEND,
> *Your kindness eased my hunger and fed my spirit when I thought all hope was gone. If Christmas prayers are answered, my humble gift will reach your hands.*
> *In deepest gratitude,*
> ELIJAH HAINES

"Elijah Haines," I whispered to the sky. Elijah Haines, my Mr. Sparrow, was alive and well.

I stared at the paper, at the flowing script, at the signature of the man who till now had no name. Then I lifted the note.

Lying against the silver bottom, wings stretched in flight, was a seagull carved from cedar. I turned the delicate figure, tracing curves and feathers that Mr. Sparrow's hands had shaped.

He wanted me to have this.

He came back to the seawall to thank me for the biscuits I'd slipped into his tin that long-ago morning.

He called me *Friend*.

I looked out over the bay and saw real flesh-and-blood seagulls silhouetted against the evening sky. I watched them glide and circle, remembering the first time I'd seen the gray-and-white birds, the first time I'd heard their calls. Their cries had stirred a lonesome, empty feeling in me, like I'd lost a piece of myself I might not ever find again.

But now they just sounded like home.